CW00822483

An Outrageous Masquerade

By the same author

TENDER DECEPTION
ISLAND FOR FIONA
ROMANCE IN RAVENDALE
HAUNTED BY SANDRA
HEARTBREAK AT HAVERSHAM
WAITING FOR MATT
MISTRESS OF CALVERLEY
A DISGRACEFUL DECEIT
A WAYWARD MISS
THE SCHEMING MR CLEEVE

An Outrageous Masquerade

Gillian Kaye

ROBERT HALE · LONDON

© Gillian Kaye 2001
First published in Great Britain 2001

ISBN 0 7090 6847 6

Robert Hale Limited
Clerkenwell House
Clerkenwell Green
London EC1R 0HT

The right of Gillian Kaye to be identified as
author of this work has been asserted by her
in accordance with the Copyright, Designs and
Patents Act 1988.

2 4 6 8 10 9 7 5 3 1

Typeset in 11/16pt Garamond
Derek Doyle & Associates, Liverpool.
Printed in Great Britain by
St Edmundsbury Press Ltd, Bury St Edmunds, Suffolk.
Bound by Woolnough Bookbinders Ltd

An Outrageous Masquerade

ONE

ON THE EDGE of Paris in the year 1794, Maxine knew real fear for the first time in her short life. She was seven years of age, tall for her years and slender, though not yet pretty. Her dark curls, cut now very close to her head, were from her father the Comte de Rochefort, but the pale-blue eyes were from her mother. The wife of the *comte* was formerly the Lady Sophia Lidiard, a young English beauty.

The de Rochefort's Paris house was not large, but the acres around it belonged to them and the *comte* was proud of his inheritance. Maxine had been born into a happy family and not alone, for there was Max her brother who was just three years older than herself.

Max and Maxine. The two children laughed often at their parents' choice of names and yet there might have been a visionary purpose in the naming. Their childhood had not been trouble free for storm clouds of revolution gathered over Paris. The Bastille had fallen in 1789 and by 1793, Louis XVI and Queen Marie Antoinette had both been executed.

Now, under Robespierre and his Committee of Public Safety, there was terror in the hearts of many noble families as thousands went to the guillotine. Many had fled to Holland, into Austria and Germany and over the English Channel to be warmly received and sheltered in England's noble houses.

The Comte de Rochefort had stood firm; he was known to be an enemy of Robespierre and he believed his life had been spared thus far because of his English wife. Sophia had borne their troubles cheerfully and had given precise instructions as to what her two children must do if the mob came their way.

That morning, Maxine was remembering her mother's words so often repeated. 'If you hear rough voices at the door and your Papa and I are taken away, you must dress in an old suit and run down the garden to Pierre's cottage and be a brave girl.' Pierre was the gardener and Maxine loved him.

And now she did hear the rough voices at the gate, the shouts of the mob. She saw her mother hastily make Max put on one of the servants' dresses, but before the *comtesse* had time to tie back his hair with a ribbon, they were surrounded.

Maxine felt the strong arms of her father around her and heard his loving, unfaltering voice. 'Be a brave girl, Maxine, and do just as Mama has told you.'

And then the wetness of her mother's tears as the *comtesse* took her silver cross and chain from her own neck and slipped it over Maxine's head with a courageous and loving whisper, 'Run to Pierre quickly. *Adieu ma chérie.*'

Then the awesome silence of the house as the Rochefort family were put on to the tumbril to be taken away to the guillotine.

She did not cry. She had an instinct to save her own life. So she clutched the bag which contained the old trousers, shirt and jacket and ran as fast as she could out of the house. She did not even stop to see if Mme Lebecque was still there in the kitchen, but opened the back door and did not stop running until she came to Pierre's cottage. He was at the door and gathered her into his arms.

Pierre Jounot had been the de Rochefort's gardener for nearly forty years and loved the family he served so faithfully. He held the small girl close to him and knew that the worst had come.

'*Ma petite*,' he said. 'Do not cry, I will keep you safe.'

For by now, the small body was racked with sobs. 'Mama and Papa and poor Max dressed like a girl. They have gone, Pierre, I will never see them again.' He could feel the tautness in her body as she clung to him and then continued courageously, 'But I won't cry any more. I must be brave for them. And Pierre, Mama says that I must change into a little boy. She says it will be safer for me if I am to stay with you. Will you have me as a little boy? And she has given me her chain and cross which she always wore round her neck.' These last words came rather proudly.

He gave her a hug and drew her into the small living-room of his cottage. Pierre had never married and to the two de Rochefort children had been as the grandfather they had never known, the *comte*'s father having died before they were born and Lady Sophia's parents far away in England.

It had been Pierre who had taught them the names of the flowers and trees, made them listen to the sounds of the birds and introduced them to the ways of the small animals about the estate. And it was Pierre who had put them on their first ponies and, not trusting them to the stable boys, had taught them to ride.

Now he looked at the small girl left to him without her family; he would guard her with his life. Then he found himself smiling as she came down the stairs in the old pair of trousers and a grey shirt of Max's, very plain and with no frills. She looked solemn, her eyes were sad, but with her short hair and long, rather serious, face, she looked the boy her parents had wished her to be.

'Would Mama be pleased with me, Pierre?' And even as she said the words, the tears trickled down her cheeks. 'Mama is in

Heaven,' she faltered, and then added with words beyond her years, 'Her earthly troubles are over. I will live with you as Max and by the time I am grown up, perhaps Paris will be a nice place once again. I hope they send that wicked Robespierre to the guillotine for he deserves to die.'

'Hush, *ma petite*,' whispered Pierre. 'You must never say such things even if they are what you believe. Come, we will go and see what Mme Lebecque has to spare for us. You will eat some supper, Maxine. . . ? No, I must get used to calling you Max from now on.'

'I don't want to think about Max,' she replied in a small voice. 'He was my friend as well as my brother.'

Her hand in his, they walked back into the house to find it deserted. The de Rochefort's good cook, Mme Lebecque, had been prepared and there was a note for Pierre to say she had gone to her son's house in Choisy just outside Paris. There was a shaky scrawl at the bottom of the note to tell him to take care of *la pauvre petite*.

Maxine was wide-eyed and shaken as she walked round the empty rooms.

'Even the servants have gone, Pierre.' She turned to him and flung her arms around his legs. 'I wish they had taken me as well; is that wicked? I believe that Mama thought they wouldn't take Max if he was dressed as a girl, but he hasn't come back, has he? I am really trying to be brave but I want to cry . . . oh, Pierre.'

He let her cry then; he thought the shed tears would help relieve the feelings that no girl as young as Maxine should have to bear. He sought desperately in his mind for something to distract her. 'Maxine, you are not alone. You have me and there are your cousins in England. Perhaps I could take you there one day.'

She looked up at him, her interest caught but only momentarily. 'I know we have cousins, but my grandmama disapproved of Mama marrying a French count. She said it would bring trouble and it has. But it is nice to know that she is there, maybe I will meet her one day. . . .' She stopped speaking as she saw a smile come into his face. 'What is it, Pierre? Have you thought of something?'

'I've remembered the kittens,' he said.

'Kittens? What kittens? Whatever are you talking about?'

Pierre picked up the bag of bread and food he had been collecting and seized the small girl by the hand.

'Come along,' he said. 'Run along to the cottage with this and then I will take you to the stables.'

Curiosity is not far behind grief in a seven year old and Maxine did as she was bidden. As he watched her, Pierre thought she did indeed look like a boy, she was tall and straight and moved quickly. I suppose it must be because she has been brought up with an older brother, he told himself. And he, too, felt like crying.

In the stables, he found that the horses had been taken and that the two stable boys were missing. But he tried not to let Maxine see his emotion and took her straight to a cupboard in the rear wall.

'Open the door,' he told her.

Maxine opened the door and in an instant her troubles vanished. 'Oh, Pierre,' she gasped, as she saw the big black cat surrounded by a tumble of small kittens, some black, some tabby. 'Can I have one?'

'Look, Maxine, this little tabby one is not doing as well as his bigger brothers and sisters. Shall we take him and feed him up? He is old enough to leave his mother.'

Pierre bent down, picked up the bundle of fur and placed it in willing arms. Maxine's expression was a mixture of all things:

11

guilt that she should feel joy at such a time; a maternal longing that here was something that needed help more than she did. And then there was the delight of feeling the soft warm fur under her fingers.

'Can I really have her? Will she be mine?' she asked. 'I will call her Marie Antoinette.'

Pierre laughed then. 'Maxine, you must not let people hear you say that name. In any case, the kitten is a male so you must think of something else.'

He saw her screw up her nose. 'I can't call him Pierre, we would get muddled up and I suppose I'd better not have Louis either if you say that is dangerous. I will think of something important . . . I know, I will call him Caesar. We have been doing about Julius Caesar in history with M. Chardin. . . .' Her voice broke. 'Oh, Pierre, he must not come. What shall we do?'

M. Chardin was the children's tutor. He was scholarly, correct and very attached to Max in particular whom he had taught since the boy first learned his letters. He lived in a small house not very far away, but Pierre knew that it would dangerous even to be seen taking Maxine out – even to leave a message with the tutor.

'*Tais-tois, ma petite*,' he said to Maxine thoughtfully. 'M. Chardin will have been told what has befallen the de Rochefort family and I don't think he will come. But, just in case, I will write a message for him and give it to a boy who is passing. A few centimes will do the trick.'

Maxine seemed satisfied, but the conversation had set the gardener thinking. It was easy enough for him to take care of a small child like Maxine dressed as his grandson, but what of the future? With inward despair he realized that it was a problem too big to contemplate. The future must take care of itself, he pondered, I must concentrate on keeping Maxine safe.

Pierre had the innate wisdom of the countryman and for the

next few days, he did his utmost to keep Maxine both occupied and interested; too tired out at the end of the day to lie awake in sorrow thinking of those she had lost.

In the few days Maxine was to be with Pierre, she tried to make herself put her misfortunes, and those of her family, behind her. She rarely laughed and she followed Pierre in earnest; he had obtained horses and she rode with him every morning, catching rabbits – and then preparing them for the pot; gathering up baskets full of logs which Pierre had sawn up ready to be used on the kitchen range. Then, in her few spare moments, pulling a ball of wool for a mischievous Caesar who seemed to have doubled in size since Maxine had had the care of him.

Caesar slept at night close to Maxine in her small bed. Pierre did not approve, but did not have the heart to say that the kitten must be kept outside in the woodshed. The time for that would come, he would think, but tried to stop himself from worrying about future years when Maxine would be growing into a young lady and no longer the boy she had become.

On a fine morning in late May, Pierre's worries came to an end and Maxine's world changed for ever when a stranger came riding through fields at the back of the house.

It was Maxine who saw him first and she ran inside to find Pierre, clinging fearfully to him. 'Pierre, come quickly . . . it is a man . . . riding . . . do you think he is coming for me? Is it my turn? Shall I hide?'

But Pierre did not even have time to reply for a voice came in halting French. 'The Comte de Rochefort, is he here? Or the *comtesse*?'

Pierre sent Maxine running up the stairs while he stepped outside. A strange sight met his eyes. The man sitting astride his horse was a very large man; he had a fine head of dark hair; his features were both handsome and young, though in a heavy kind of way. But it was his dress which gave cause for astonishment. Though obviously a gentleman, he was wearing a loose coat and breeches of rough brown woollen cloth with the black worsted waistcoat and stockings of the farm labourer.

'This is the house of the Comte de Rochefort?' he asked again and Pierre knew that he was not confronting a fellow-country-man.

'What do you want with the *comte*?' he asked suspiciously and, without realizing it, in the English so carefully learned from the *comtesse*.

The stranger jumped from the horse and seemed even taller when standing up straight. Pierre was a tall man himself but felt dwarfed.

'Dammit, you speak English. Who are you?'

'*M'sieur*, I am Pierre Jounot, gardener to the late Comte de Rochefort.'

He felt a hand grip his soulder and the grip was urgent.

'Do you say "late". Is the *comte* not still alive? Do not tell me I have come in vain.' The stranger sounded put out. 'You had better tell me their fate.'

Pierre directed him into the cottage and watched him bow his head in the low doorway. 'Sit down, *m'sieur*, and I will fetch you some ale.'

'Thank you, it would be welcome, I have ridden hard this morning.'

In all this time, Maxine had been crouched down at the top of the stairway. She could not see the visitor but listened eagerly to every word. She had an odd presentiment that this man, speaking so much like her mother when she had used her native English, had come seeking her.

'Are we safe here?' was the stranger's first question.

'*M'sieur*, I do not know who you are, but I must tell you that tragedy has struck the de Rochefort family. The house is deserted and we will not see the likes of the mob again. I was spared and so was the little . . . Max.'

'Max?'

'Yes, the *comte*'s youngest child, he is safe here with me.' Pierre said quietly, not wishing to disclose that there was a young girl in the house until he knew who the stranger was. He was certain by now that the unexected visitor was an English gentleman in spite of the rough clothing.

'We are too late.' The words were solemn and followed by a long silence. 'I must explain who I am and what is my purpose in coming here.' Again he was silent as though he was gathering his thoughts together.

'The Comtesse de Rochfort was my aunt though she was in fact almost a contemporary of mine. You see my father was the second eldest son in the family and Sophia was the youngest; there were nearly twenty years between them. I always called her Sophia and when she married the Comte de Rochefort, I was quite a young man. I remember well my grandmother's disaproval of the match and I am sorry to say that once Sophia had established herself in Paris, they lost touch.' He paused and looked at the older man sitting across the table from him. 'You must know that in England, we have been much disturbed by the troubles in France. Many of your noble families fled to England and I always had the feeling that my grandmother hoped and hoped that she would see Sophia again . . . you look puzzled, Pierre. I may call you Pierre?'

'You speak of your grandmother, *m'sieur*, but surely she must be quite an elderly lady by now?'

The visitor smiled for the first time. 'She is over sixty but she is a very strong and forceful lady – she is the dowager countess, you know – and she insists on living on her own when she could quite easily have had a home with her eldest son. She is very proud and I think she is now regretting her pride. She will certainly do so when I return with the news of her daughter's death. It was the guillotine, Pierre? May I ask when?'

Pierre relied quietly. 'Just over a week ago.'

'Goddammit, I came as soon as she asked me. You will wonder why I am dressed as a farm labourer?' he said.

'I think it is good sense, *m'sieur*.'

'Yes, I did not think it would be wise to be seen dressed as an English gentleman.'

'Would you like to tell me your name and the purpose of your visit?' Pierre asked politely.

'I am George Lidiard. As I said, my father was the second son of the Earl and Countess Hampton; he died some years ago and my mother is living with one of my sisters. I live on my own in the house my father inherited, but please do not think that I am wealthy. A second son does not bring riches and I consider myself fortunate in having a small estate.'

'And you hoped to persuade the *comte* and *comtesse* to return to England with you?' Pierre asked.

George Lidiard nodded. 'We heard of the Terror and the executions under Robespierre and my grandmother begged me to come and try to bring the family back to England. She has secured the use of a fine sailing vessel and I have it moored near Cherbourg.' He put his hands to his head. 'It is all in vain. I think it will break Grandmama's heart.'

'The *comte* would not have come,' said Pierre soberly. 'He loved his country and was a staunch royalist. I think that it was only the fact of the *comtesse* being an Englishwoman that kept him from being sent to the guillotine at the same time as King Louis . . . I think though that he might have let his children go to England.'

16

'Tell me about the children – they have the same Lidiard blood in their veins as I do myself. Do I remember you saying that the youngest boy was here with you?'

Pierre nodded. 'There were two children. The elder was ten years old and sadly taken with the *comte* and *comtesse*. Max, the younger, was hidden here with me. I sent him upstairs when I heard you approach.'

The Englishman stood up, strain vanished from his face to be replaced with hope. 'What would happen to him if he remained here? What are your intentions? You are not a young man.'

A sorrowful look came over Pierre's face. 'I have been so much occupied with keeping young Max from grieving that I have given no thought to the future. It is too awful to contemplate. What do you suggest, *m'sieur*?'

The man who was first cousin to Maxine became suddenly decisive. 'I will take him back with me and bring him up as my son. I am not yet married but I can offer him a home. The Dowager Countess Hampton will be pleased and I must tell you that my uncle, Thomas Lidiard, who is the sixth earl, has a large family. His eldest son is married and living with him at Lidiard Manor; his young family will be company for Max de Rochefort. What will the child think, Pierre?'

Pierre was torn. 'I will hate to lose him but it is proper that he should be with his family if you can get him safely back to England. Shall I call him?'

'Yes, please.'

Pierre went to the foot of the wooden stairs that led to the two small bedrooms.

'Max, come quickly, it is safe. The rider you saw was an Englishman and is a kinsman of yours.'

Slowly Maxine came down the stairs. She had heard the conversation and her cousin's suggestion, but she felt no excitement at the thought of being taken from the only home she knew. And she did not want to leave Pierre.

She was clutching Caesar to her and tears were not far away. In the small living-room, she found herself looking up a long way to the handsome face of her burly cousin. She took an instant dislike to him. His eyes were as blue as her own and his hair as dark, but his face was slightly bloated making his eyes seem small and with an expression she did not like.

'I am not leaving Pierre.' Her voice was no more than a growl of obstinancy.

'You are Max de Rochefort? You have been listening to our conversation?' As there was no reply, George Lidiard continued. 'I have to introduce myself as your cousin and tell you that your grandmama has sent me to take you safely back to England. I am sorry I have arrived too late to save your parents.'

'My father would not have gone with you. He has died for France.' Maxine spoke proudly and he frowned.

'And your mama?'

'She would always do as Papa asked her,' she said clearly.

'I believe that they would be pleased to think that you were safely in England with your mama's family.'

Maxine looked at Pierre who was nodding sadly. '*Ma petite*, it is not right for you to be brought up by your father's gardener. I do not wish to lose you, but if you will go with your cousin then I will travel to Dijon and live with my sister. I will know you are safe, you see.'

'One moment,' interrupted the Englishman. 'Why did you call the lad "*ma petite*"? I know enough French to know that it is what you would call a small girl.'

Pierre looked both startled and guilty, but looking at Maxine's face, he saw a little grin which spoke of both triumph and amusement.

'I am waiting for an answer,' said the large gentleman with some impatience.

Maxine stepped up to him. She was still cuddling the sleeping kitten in her arms. When she spoke she sounded much older than her years. 'Cousin, if that is what you are, you see I cannot come to live with you. I am dressed as a boy because Mama thought it was more sensible if I was going to be with Pierre. But I am a girl and my name is Maxine: it would be quite improper for me to grow up as a young lady in your household if you have no wife.'

George Lidiard looked at the intelligent face and bright expression; she was right, damn her, and he could see her growing into a handful of a young madam with those bright blue eyes and sharp French wit about her. But wait, he was saying to himself, in ten years' time she will be a young beauty and ready to be wed. And by that time, I will be nearly forty and ready to settle down and rear a family. Why not? He was of a sensual nature and anyone who knew him well would have seen him relishing the prospect of such a ravishing young bride.

But he gave no hint of his thoughts and answered Maxine reassuringly. 'Cousin Maxine, you speak the truth. We will keep you as a boy for a while and I will call you Max. No one will know our secret and it will save the expense of having to procure a lady companion for you.' George Lidiard was known in his family for being a mean-fisted man and although Maxine did not know it, he was showing his true colours. He continued, looking at her closely, 'Does that suit you? Do you like being a boy?'

Maxine looked at Pierre and he nodded. 'Yes, I do, for it means that I will not have to ride side-saddle. I used to ride astride when I was out with Max. . . .' She faltered over the name and drew a deep breath. 'Max was my older brother who went to the guillotine with Mama and Papa. Perhaps I will not miss him so much if I have cousins nearby as I heard you telling Pierre.'

'Yes, your Uncle Thomas has grandchildren nearer to your age. Will you be able to pretend?'

She nodded. 'Oh yes, I am used to pretending to be Max when we were in a scrape. He always said that I was as good as any boy ... I cannot believe he has gone, you know, it seems like a bad dream.'

The hard heart of George Lidiard was touched and he stepped close to the girl. 'We will do very well, Maxine, and that is the last time I shall call you by that name. My aunt and her *comte* did not show much imagination when they named you.

'No, it was a joke to Max and me, but sometimes it was useful.'

'Yes, I can imagine it was,' replied her cousin. 'And what is that you have in your arms?'

'He is Caesar,' Maxine replied defensively. 'He is mine, I will not be parted from him.'

'But we cannot take him on horseback all the way to Cherbourg.'

'Then I will not go.'

She has a will of her own, this one, said George to himself, but I had better humour her. 'Get Pierre to pack a bag for you, then Caesar can lie on the top. You will have to ride in front of me.'

Maxine frowned. 'Very well,' she said. 'Will you go to your sister's straight away, Pierre?'

'Almost, Maxine, as soon as I have seen to your father's affairs.'

George Lidiard looked at him keenly. 'How has the estate been settled, Pierre, do you know?'

'The *comte* told me in case this very thing should happen. He was well prepared. The property will be sold and all his fortune is to be settled in a London bank for Max. But, of course, I have to write and tell the lawyers that Maxine is now the heir so it will eventually come to her.' He looked at the Englishman and thought he could see a greedy glint in his eyes and added hastily, 'And that will be when she comes of age I should think.' Pierre stopped, visibly upset by what he was having to say, but he would not let Maxine see him falter. 'He and the *comtesse* would have been happy to know that Maxine was to be taken safely to her relatives in England. The *comtesse* always regretted the coolness between herself and her mother.'

Maxine was staring at her tall cousin; it was as though something had suddenly occurred to her. 'How do we know that you really are a Lidiard and not a spy for Robespierre?' she shot at him.

George Lidiard almost laughed at her serious and pointed question. How old was this child? Her experience at the hands of the Committee of Public Safety had given her a wisdom beyond her years. He put his hand into the large pocket of his riding coat.

'I had almost forgotten, Maxine . . . I am sorry, I must remember to say Max. Your grandmama wrote a letter to her daughter. I will give it to you. You read English? You certainly speak it very well.'

'Mama made sure we could speak English just as she did, but always, we conversed in French. I know both, you see. Can I have the letter?' She took a large sheet of paper from him and read the closely written words out loud.

My dearest Sophia

The news from France gets worse every day and I cannot let our disagreement continue. I am sending this note by your brother George's son, Mr George Lidiard. If you will come, he is willing to escort you to England where you will be welcome to make a home with me. In the event of you insisting to stand fast by your husband the comte, which is your duty, do not hesitate to send your children. We will keep them safe until these terrible times are over and there is peace between France and England.

I hope George reaches you in time.

Your loving mother

Georgiana, Dowage Countess Hampton

Tears trickled down Maxine's face and she hastily brushed them away. I am a little girl no longer, she made herself think.

'Cousin George,' she said, as though she was seventeen and not seven years of age, 'it is kind of my grandmother and I know that my mama would have wished me to go to England. She will rest in peace if I am there. So, yes, I am prepared to come to your yacht with you. When do you wish to start?'

George must have had the same feelings for he bent towards her and spoke kindly. 'If Pierre can provide us with a lunch then we will set off straight away and hope to be in Cherbourg before nightfall. Is there anything you wish to take from the house?'

'Nothing,' she replied. 'I am going to a new country and a new life and have no wish to be reminded of the sadness of these last years.'

'Well said, Max, you have courage and I admire you. I think that you and I will deal well together for the next few years.'

'I hope so,' she said politely, but there was something about him which gave her an uneasiness. She thought it was too vague to be called dislike and she must make the most of his kindness.

She had very little to pack and after a substantial lunch of rabbit stew, Maxine made Caesar comfortable on the top of her bag and let Pierre help her up on to her cousin's horse.

She hugged Pierre briefly before he lifted her up and struggled to keep herself from crying. 'Thank you for looking after me,

Pierre, and please go to your sister soon.'

She settled herself astride the horse and felt the reassurance and solid figure of her cousin behind her.

'*Adieu*, Pierre,' she called out and to her cousin. 'Please, go quickly.'

TWO

*F*OR EVER AFTERWARDS, Maxine found that her memory of the next few hours and the following days was extremely hazy. Certain things stood clear in her mind as though they were isolated and disconnected incidents.

The *Sunrise* she remembered not at all, but the grey swell of the English Channel as they crossed swiftly to Weymouth seemed as an echo of calm in a troubled world.

She remembered her cousin's strong arm about her on his horse and his words when they reached the coast. 'I am taking you straight to your grandmama, Max; she lives with my sister, Rose, at Lidiard Grange. It is a big old house and not far from Triscombe House – that is the name of my home and it will soon be home to you. Triscombe is just outside the little Dorset village of Halstock and on the other side of the village is Lidiard Manor. That is where you will find you have cousins of your own age. Dorset is a big county in the West of England and I am sure you will soon grow to like it there.'

Strange names dropped quite kindly by Cousin George, yet she remembered not the journey, nor the coach from Weymouth to her grandmother's. Just the names: Dorset, Lidiard, Halstock, Manor, Grange, Triscombe. They were almost magical to her ear even when later they became an integral part of her life.

Then she found herself in front of her grandmama and there were seconds of awe. The elderly lady was all in black except for a cross of silver around her neck and a ruff of white lace. The dowager's hair was white, too, but her cap was of a flimsy black. She stood tall and unsmiling and Maxine never forgot the word that came into her young mind – fearsome.

She had with her a younger woman who fluttered in the background and Maxine learned later that this was her Cousin Rose and sister to George. Rose had never married and was of a timid nature, but she was kind-hearted and attentive and seemed to enjoy her position as her grandmother's companion and helpmeet.

When the dowager spoke, there was a ghost of a smile and a kindly word and Maxine's world changed.

'You are Max, my Sophia's Max. Did you want to come to England?'

'Yes, please, Grandmama.'

'I would have you here but it would be no life for a child, though I do have dear Rose with me, she is such a help. Go with your cousin George, you will have the freedom of the estate and when you grow up, you can help him. And your cousins are nearby. My eldest son, Thomas – he is the sixth earl – has his grandchildren living at Lidiard Manor and they will be about your age. . . .' She turned to her grandson. 'George, I will not grieve for Sophia, that is all in the past. Max will replace her in my affections; he has her blue eyes. Take care of him.'

A short journey and they arrived at Triscombe House. Maxine immediately felt at home; she had a first impression of a small, compact house of cream stone which appeared warm and welcoming.

'Here we are, Max, this is Triscombe House,' said her cousin as they approached the handsome building. 'It is my home and I hope that it will be yours for many years. Mrs Turnbull is my cook and housekeeper and I trust you will always be polite to her. I have decided that it would be wise to tell her of your true circumstances. If you are to grow up here, she would soon learn the truth of your being a girl. But only Mrs Turnbull, no one else. You must always remember that no one will know that you are really Maxine, you will be a boy to everyone you meet.'

And then the heart-warming impression that never left Maxine in all the following years. The large, comfortable, kindly Mrs Turnbull who took one look at the newcomer and said, 'My word, what a big girl to travel all that way. You can be certain that your secret will be safe with me. Do you understand English? If not, I'll soon teach you.'

It was Cousin George who laughed heartily. 'Max speaks English as well as you or me, Mrs Turnbull, my Aunt Sophia saw to that. God rest her soul.'

Ten years went by and for Maxine, they were not unhappy ones. This was largely due to the circumstance of Thomas Lidiard, sixth Earl of Hampton, living with his son and his grandchildren so near to Triscombe House.

Maxine found herself living on the edge of Halstock with Lidiard Manor not a stone's throw away on the other side of the village.

And Lidiard Manor soon came to mean something special to Maxine; this was due to her friendship with her cousins, Humphrey and Walter Lidiard. They were the grandsons of the sixth earl and only a few years older than Maxine. They had sisters who were not a lot more than babies and still in the nursery, so Maxine was able to remain Max quite easily with the company she kept. The boys' father insisted that Max should share their tutor, and, daily, she would ride the short distance from Triscombe House to Lidiard Manor.

It was never questioned that she was not a boy. It pleased her that she had grown up tall and very slender, with a long and serious face which lightened into smiles only when she was with her cousins.

For there were not many smiles in evidence at Triscombe House. She never grew to like Cousin George and she soon discovered the reasons for that very first instinctive distrust of him when he had arrived in Paris.

In the same ten years that she had grown up happily with her cousins at Lidiard Manor, George had gone from thirty to forty years of age. And in Maxine's eyes, he had not changed. She soon found him to be mean with his money and neglectful of his estate.

The household was kept sparingly by the careful Mrs Turnbull, and George had nothing to spend on Maxine's education. The earl supplied her first ponies and then, when she was old enough, with a fine mare from his own stables. Even her clothes were passed on as her cousins grew out of them though Maxine had no objection to this as only the best was bought for Humphrey and Walter. She knew that if Cousin George had had the dressing of her, she would have gone very shabbily indeed.

And he did not care about his land or the tenant farmers who eked out miserable lives in the two farm cottages. As Maxine passed from child to young woman, she found her sympathies were with the Triscombe tenants rather than with her cousin.

As she grew to understand George's character and his lifestyle, she liked him less and less. Although little was spent on the upkeep of his home, he never seemed to be short of money to spend in the gaming clubs of the popular seaside resort of Weymouth where he had a small house. He spent more on drink than on food and his rather handsome face became florid as he reached his fortieth year. Indeed, from the gossip she had heard and the pictures and caricatures she had seen, Maxine thought that her cousin was not unlike that other George who was Prince of Wales and not far from George Lidiard in age and habits.

But it was his reputation in the neighbourhood for romantic attachments to certain wealthy widowed ladies that gave cause for scandal. And, Maxine, as she approached her seventeenth birthday, knew that no pretty servant girl was safe from his rakish ways and many had left Triscombe House in tears because they were expecting his child.

These were the things that gave the young Maxine a dislike of her cousin and it was a dislike that was coupled with fear as to what would happen to her when this masquerade as a young man would come to an end as it must do soon.

By the year 1804 – the year in which Napoleon was crowned Emperor in Paris – Maxine found herself once again jolted out of what had seemed a trouble-free life. The events which were to lead to her change of fortune in that year started when her cousins Humphrey and Walter went off to Oxford for their degrees.

Left alone, she found herself more in the company of Cousin George and this gave her cause for anxiety. In June and not far from her seventeenth birthday, her cousin's elderly steward died. Amos Duntish had been nearly eighty years of age and long since incapable of carrying out his duties about the estate.

Maxine, respecting his advancing years, had helped wherever she was able and became quite fond of the old countryman. As she and her cousin walked back from Amos's funeral in Halstock church, she was wondering what George would do about replacing his steward. She even wondered if her cousin would replace him at all, and leave his tenants in even poorer circumstances.

It was barely one hundred yards from Halstock church to Triscombe House and George had not bothered with his carriage, He walked the leafy Dorset lane, Maxine tall and straight by his side.

'What will you do about a new steward, Cousin George?' she asked.

He looked down at her, ignoring her question and thinking only of what his next move would be. Forever conscious of the feminity beneath her boyish looks, he spoke to her with a relish which did not at first disclose his aim to obtain her as his wife.

'It is not so much of poor old Amos I am thinking, Max.'

Maxine looked up quickly. She was dressed faultlessly in a dark grey cutaway coat over a paler grey pantaloons and hessians; her waistcoat was black and in no way revealed her feminine form; her neckcloth was very modest. Her dark hair still curled but it was cut close to the head and in some ways, made her look younger than her seventeen years.

'What do you mean, Cousin?' she asked quickly.

'It will soon be your seventeenth birthday, Max,' he smiled, and the look in his eyes seemed to search beneath the black waistcoat and made her feel uncomfortable.

'In a few days' time,' she replied quietly.

'I think you might become Maxine on that day, my dear.'

Maxine stopped in her tracks; they had just reached Triscombe House and were standing within the wrought-iron gates at the end of the short drive. In all the years she had spent with her cousin, she had dreaded the time when she would have to change into dresses and gowns and become a lady. And now, listening to her cousin's words, she feared to think of what thoughts lay behind them.

'I would rather stay as Max, Cousin,' she replied shortly.

His hand reached out and lay lightly and somehow caressingly on her arm. 'But I cannot have Max as my wife,' he said smoothly.

Maxine jerked away from him and stood facing him squarely, her temper flaring and her blue eyes both alarmed and indignant.

'What are you talking about? I am not going to become your

wife, not ever. I know that one day I will have to become a young lady, but that need not be for four or five years, I hope.'

George Lidiard admired her spirit and it made him more determined than ever to make her his own as soon as possible, even if it meant he would have to give up the delectable Diana who stayed waiting in Weymouth to tempt him. Or do I have to give her up, he said to himself? Maxine need not know.

'I think you must do as I wish, Maxine – there you are, I have used your name – I brought you to Triscombe House with the intention of making you my bride one day.'

Maxine was outraged. 'I was only seven years of age when I came here, how can you have thought of such a thing? Your sentiments do you no credit, Cousin. I will never become your wife not even if I have to live the rest of my life as Max de Rochefort. . . .' She stopped in her tirade as his hold on her arm became as a band of steel.

'You will do as I say, Maxine. Have I not kept you in comfort all these years, almost as though you were my son? Do you feel no sense of gratitude towards me for taking you away from the horrors of Paris?' His tone was cool.

She tried to control her temper. 'Of course I am grateful to you, and I love Dorset and I love my cousins. But your wife? Never. You must be old enough to be the father you are pretending you have been. It is like talking about . . . incest.' She flung the word at him and then regretted it for an ugly look came into his eyes.

His grip on her arm tightened until she cried out with the pain. 'Maxine, you know very well that you are only a cousin to me, the relationship is not a close one. Underneath that sober waistcoat you are wearing for poor old Amos, lies a soft breast, a tender heart. They will both be mine very soon, I believe.'

Maxine flung his hand away from her. 'I find you disgusting,

Cousin, please do not mention the matter again. I had rather take Amos's place as your steward than become your wife.'

He laughed at her then and put his hands on her shoulders. She recoiled thinking he was going to kiss her.

He read her thoughts. 'No, I am not going to kiss you, do not fear. I can wait for your kisses; perhaps one day you will be of a mind to give them willingly. But you have given me an idea. I do believe it would suit me to have you as my steward for a few years. It would save me Amos's wage. Would you like it, Maxine – no, on consideration I must call you Max again – would you indeed like to become my steward? I believe you know Amos's ways already for you have helped him often enough. Do not think I have not noticed. Yes, Max, be my steward and I will make you Maxine when you are five-and-twenty. After all, by that time we will have the benefit of your inheritance.'

Maxine felt such a relief that she had escaped the immediate threat of marriage to her loathesome cousin, that his last words went unheeded though she knew that George had established from the lawyers that she inherited her father's fortune at the age of twenty-five. She would remain Max and enjoy doing a steward's work around the estate. It would do no harm to stay out of petticoats for a few more years.

And so she took a deep breath and spoke very seriously. 'Is it agreed then, Cousin? I will be your steward from this day and you will forget the ridiculous notion of me becoming your wife. I am sure you will find someone far more suitable before long.'

George gave a slight bow towards her. 'It is agreed, Cousin, and I am sure that if you need the proper kind of breeches and jacket for the task, then my cousin at Lidiard Manor will be able to help you.'

Maxine nodded and started to walk towards the house. 'I am sure he will, Cousin George, he has always been most generous.'

The last words were said very deliberately, but the irony of them was lost on George Lidiard. He arrived at his home satisfied that he had not only secured a new steward who would cost him nothing, but that he would have the pleasure of a union with his cousin in a few years' time. He somehow thought that she would be a beauty by then.

Maxine slipped easily into her new task. Her roan mare, Liddy – named so because she came from the Lidiard stables – took her around the estate which was not a large one. The land was rolling pasture with the heathland of Dorset as its boundary; both cattle and sheep did well, and the arable land brought in enough fodder for the animals and corn to send to the mill. The lambs were sold at Dorchester market which was less than ten miles away.

Maxine already knew the tenants of the two farms and she recognized that it was here that her greatest problem would lie. There were the Lockyers at Downs Farm and the Grattans at The Elms. Both farms were well named for the Lockyers's farm lay alongside the chalk downland which was a feature of that part of Dorset.

It was here that Maxine loved to ride; and especially so when the fits of lonely sadness overcame her at the thought of her lost family. At these times, it was Max in particular she remembered for she knew that he, too, would have loved a gallop over the downs. He used to challenge her to a race to the nearest clump of trees on the de Rochefort estate. She had been but seven years of age and she always lost the race but she never took it to heart for the joy of seeing the triumphant smile on Max's face as he galloped away from her.

The Elms was the farm nearest to the house and the one visited most by Maxine. The old farmhouse had been built in the shelter of a group of tall elms and had stood at that spot for 200 years.

Maxine made her first visit to The Elms on the day after Amos's funeral. She knew that the Grattans would be wondering what was to become of them under a new steward. She rode up the farm track and left Liddy by one of the barns; it was but a step to the cottage and she found herself looking at it with a critical eye. The thatch was a bad colour and bare in places, falling in a ragged manner where it met the eaves of the building; many of the windows were cracked or broken and the once sturdy front door sagged on its hinges. How can Cousin George let it get into such a state, she was wondering, and whatever can I do to make the necessary repairs? He will never give me the money.

There was a smell of baking coming from the kitchen and Maxine did not knock but walked through the cluttered living-room to find Mrs Grattan busy with the weekly bake of bread.

Mrs Grattan was a dumpling of a woman; short and round and comfortable and with a ready smile in spite of her many troubles. She was standing at the floury wooden table and two small girls were on chairs and were busy kneading some dough into round shapes to make bread buns. Their brothers, two tall strong boys like their father, were helping in the fields.

If it was a shabby scene that met Maxine's eyes, it was a happy one. The girls' long smock dresses were grey and thread-bare, but their hair was curly and clean and they looked over at Maxine with delight for she was a favourite of theirs.

'Master Max,' exclaimed Mrs Grattan; it had been her name for Maxine since the flight from France and it had not changed as Maxine had grown older. 'Poor old Amos, he were a good man no mistake, even if he were past doing much these last years. I'm sure as I don't know what will happen to us now. Will your cousin be getting a new steward? He needs one bad for he don't attend to things hisself, begging your pardon, Master Max.'

Maxine stood at the end of the table and took in the scene. The kitchen was hot for the open fire was stoked up with wood faggots to heat the side-oven ready for the baking of the bread. She suspected that the bread was the Grattans' main diet helped out with the stew pot of swedes and turnips and the occasional rabbit.

At the end of the table was the ladder which took the Grattan family up to their bedroom which was no more than the space under the roof and housed them all in one big room divided by a curtain. Washing was done under the pump in the back yard and they lived in the front room she had just come through. Clean but ragged curtains hung at small windows and the floors were of beaten earth. It had long been a dream of Maxine's to see flag-stones laid in the cottages.

But she had to reply to Mrs Grattan. 'My cousin George is not getting another steward, Mrs Grattan. I don't know what you and Mr Grattan will say, but I am to become steward. I know I am young but I have been round with old Amos these last four years and I know what needs doing.'

Mrs Grattan was beaming. 'Why, Master Max, that be good news for us. I know you have our interests at heart and perhaps you'll be able to persuade that close-fisted cousin of yours to spend something on his cottages.'

But Maxine was shaking her head; she did not feel hopeful. 'Mrs Grattan, I will do my best, that is all I can say. I know Mr Grattan and the two boys to be good workers, and as for you, Mrs Grattan, I think that the butter that comes from your dairy is the best in the village of Halstock.'

The beam on the face of the farmer's wife grew broader but her words did not match her expression. 'It's hard, Master Max, it's hard. But Grattan be proud of his dairy herd and it's up to me to be helping where I can.' She looked at her daughters. 'And these two are growing up and will be able to help me in the dairy. If we can make more butter and sell it at Dorchester market, then perhaps I'll be able to buy a length or two of cotton to make them some new smocks. But I'm right pleased as it's you who is going to be steward, maybe things will change for the better. They couldn't be much worse.' She added the last words gloomily and lost her smile.

'I will do it somehow but it won't be overnight. Just have patience with me, Mrs Grattan, and always be sure to tell me if there is anything you need. I'll be off now and leave you to your baking. I have to ride up to Downs Farm to see the Lockyers.'

Ever since reaching Dorset at the age of seven, Maxine had been in the habit of visiting her grandmother along with her cousin. She had grown to love the old lady who in so many ways, reminded her of her own mother. The dowager lived comfortably enough at Lidiard Grange with Rose, but Maxine soon discovered that she had little fortune. She had been badly provided for by the fifth earl and Lidiard Manor and the wealth of the Lidiards had passed to Thomas, her eldest son.

At first, Maxine was puzzled by the fact that the dowager chose to live on her own when she could have been comfortable at Lidiard Manor with Thomas and the rest of her family. But as time went by, she discovered her grandmother to be a woman of exceptional independence and with opinions which would not have found much favour with the jovial and generous Thomas.

So it was that when Maxine realized that she needed money to improve the living conditions of the Grattans and the Lockyers, she could rely on neither her cousin George nor her grandmother for financial help.

After nearly five years of hard work, and still two years away from her own inheritance, she found herself falsifying the books with no conscience at all in order to provide the two farms with flagstone floors. At her wits' end to know how to repair the thatch, it took a visit to Weymouth, a quarrel with Cousin George, and the work of a highwayman to bring Maxine's masquerade as the steward of the Triscombe estate to a crisis.

THREE

*I*T WAS THE year 1809 and England was at war with France. There was fighting in Spain and in Portugal. Along the Dorset coast, preparations were made should Napoleon invade. Groups of men formed and called themselves the Local Volunteers; beacons were built of faggots and furze on hill tops across the county ready to give warning of any invasion.

But all this activity and apprehension left Maxine untouched for she had reached her twenty-second year and she knew that she could not carry on the pose of being a young man for very much longer.

Her cousin George made sly remarks about it being almost five years since he had first declared his intention of making her his wife. She found this insulting as she battled unsuccessfully with him to provide his two farms with new thatch. She had enjoyed her years as steward but there had been many worries, the greatest at the moment being how to stop the two families in the farm cottages from the soakings they received from the leaking thatch as they slept.

On top of this, she found herself the object of the adoration of Melissa, the youngest Lidiard granddaughter who was no longer in the nursery, but had grown into a lovely-looking and prettily behaved girl of seventeen. Maxine was fond of Melissa, but found the situation embarrasssing and knew that her posturing as a young man would have to come to an end very soon.

But there was an obstinacy in Maxine's nature, an independent spirit which had seen her through many awkward situations. And she made a vow to herself. 'I will not cease to be Cousin George's steward until I have provided the Grattans and the Lockyers with new thatch.' She did not know how she could do it, but was confident that she would find a way before her cousin forced her to reveal herself as a young lady.

George Lidiard was now in his mid-forties; still handsome in a florid kind of way though heavier about his body and slower in his movements. He still dallied with the beautiful and faithful Diana whom he had now installed in his Weymouth house. But he was aware that the sands of time were running against him and he must soon secure Maxine as his wife. It had amused him to see her acting out the masquerade as his steward for the last five years; in that time, he thought that she had become very good-looking and that under the sober tweeds she wore about the estate, he would find an abundant and fruitful figure.

He took little notice of her pleas for thatch or a new plough, for broken windows to be mended; she did her duty in collecting the rents and that was all that bothered him. He too, had noticed the little Melissa casting beseeching looks at Maxine. Soon he would have to arrange matters to his advantage.

It was Maxine's habit to accompany her cousin into Dorchester on most market days; he would find a few cronies for whist, faro or some other gambling game while Maxine enjoyed meeting up with the farmers and stewards from the county. It amused her that they accepted her as one of them; even her abstemious habits with the local ale did not arouse their suspicions. She was regarded as a handsome, clever youth doing his best for the unpopular George Lidiard.

On these occasion, Maxine and George would have a late dinner in the town and it would be almost dark before they started home for Halstock.

One fine September market day found the two cousins journeying back from Dorchester just as the sun was going down; the evening had the first chill of the approaching autumn. Samuel-coachman was in good form having spent most of the day drinking with his fellow coachmen. He took the carriage at a spanking pace completely ignoring the fact that old Prince was more used to a steady plod, and he did not heed that the trees along the road were already casting their dark shadows over the Dorset landscape.

Inside the carriage, George was equally jovial, but not quite in his cups. Maxine felt tired after the long day and was eyeing her cousin warily. His talk and his behaviour threatened to become insultingly personal.

'You are looking well today, Max; you should always wear a red waistcoat, it becomes your dark hair. Dammit if I don't feel I would like to know what lies beneath the waistcoat. . . .'

Maxine felt herself stiffen and sit tightly in her corner; the windows of the carriage were small and it was not a gracious vehicle. She was used to jests such as these from Cousin George and they normally went unheeded by her. But that evening, with not much light coming through the windows and the coach swaying with Samuel-coachman's wild driving, she became aware that she could easily be thrown closer to George than she would wish to be.

'I will have none of that kind of talk, thank you, Cousin George,' she said coolly.

'Ha,' he gave a short raucous laugh. 'Maxine is pretending

primness after her day out with the farmers. How much do they know of you, Cousin?'

'They know nothing. You are well aware that you and Mrs Turnbull are the only possessors of the truth of my identity. And I have trusted you.' Even as she said the words, Maxine knew that the days of trusting her cousin were almost over.

'You can indeed trust me, my pretty one, I can enjoy what others know nothing of. Come and give me a kiss and tell me that you will soon be mine.'

He lurched to her side of the carriage and his hand slipped beneath her coat and sought to caress her through the soft scarlet waistcoat she had been so proud of.

She struck at his hand and shrank further back into her corner. As he leaned close and she began to panic, the carriage juddered to an abrupt halt; they heard a loud bang followed by a shot as from a pistol. Outside, voices were raised and George Lidiard sprang towards the door.

'Goddammit,' he blustered. 'What is going on?' He had no time to say more for the door was opened and Maxine could see, even in the dim twilight, a black mask over a swarthy face and a hand holding a pistol.

'M'lord and m'lady, hand over your rings. That'll do for a start.'

'Go to hell, you get nothing from me,' shouted George and then, in an even louder bellow. 'Samuel, where's that blunder-buss?'

A laugh reached them from the man at the door. 'Shot from out of his hand, it were. Neat I thought. I didn't shoot the coachman, that's not my way, just the blunderbuss. Now hurry up; I'll take your sovereigns and guineas if you've none of the pretty stuff on you.'

George seemed to remember Maxine for the first time. She was transfixed in her corner, half-scared, half-fascinated by the turn of events. She herself wore no jewellery and her cousin likewise.

'Max, that cross you wear round your neck. Give the fellow that,' her cousin shouted at her.

Blind rage shook Maxine. The cross on its silver chain was the one her mother had slipped over her head as the tumbril waited at the door all those years ago. Never would she be parted from such a treasure.

She struck out at George and such was his surprise that he took his attention from the pistol-holding highwayman.

'You dare touch me,' yelled Maxine in fury. 'I'll die before I give you Mama's cross.'

'That's right, milady . . . oh, pardon, it's not milady at all,' came the rough voice from the door. 'You his son then? You don't look more'n sixteen and that's the truth. I wouldn't take your cross from you; they don't call me soft-hearted Jack for nothing. You get m'lord to empty his pockets for me. It's only a few coins I'm after, just to buy me some supper and a lodging and the rest I can take home to m'wife.'

'You get nothing from me,' bellowed George and again shouted for his missing coachman. 'Samuel, where are you?'

A laugh came from the door. 'Hiding behind the horse, that's where he is and if he moves, I'll shoot him. He knows that.'

Maxine pushed past George to the dim opening. She held out her hand. 'Here's a guinea for you. Now leave us alone.'

Underneath the mask, a grin. 'Thanks, youngster,' and the fellow put out his free hand. At the same time, Maxine came closer, knocked the pistol flying and it clattered to the ground.

'Well, I'll be. . . .'

'Be quiet,' Maxine thundered, trying to keep her voice low. 'George, give me another guinea. That will do for his night's work . . . no, you needn't argue, you'll do as I say. Hurry up or he'll be picking up his pistol again. Hurry, for heaven's sake.'

George Lidiard had been drinking all day and his wits were befuddled. He stared at Maxine as though he had not seen her before. 'In my travelling coat . . .' he grunted.

He was dressed in skin-tight pantaloons and stylish jacket of deep blue – a gentleman had no way of keeping money on his person. But his caped travelling-coat was thrown on the seat between him and Maxine, and she hastily turned it over and found his purse in the capacious pocket.

Another guinea changed hands and the highwayman rode off with a cheerful quip. 'Thanks, youngster. If ever you want employment you can apply to me. Well known between Dorchester and Weymouth, I am. Lovely countryside is Dorset. . . .' The last words were lost to them and George was climbing out of the carriage to find out what had happened to Samuel-coachman and the blunderbuss.

'Samuel, where are you? The first time we've ever been held up and what use were you? We could have been killed.'

The elderly Samuel rose to his feet from behind the horse and Maxine, coming up behind George, had to smile. Samuel should have been pensioned off years ago, but she was aware that a younger man would have cost her cousin more money. Samuel stood there in his carriage coat, looking sorry for himself and rubbing his shoulder.

'Sorry, Mr George, sir, I did my best with the blunderbuss but the darn thing shot over the top of the fellow's head. And straight away, he fired it right out me hand. Look, there it is where I dropped 'un. Reckon you've got to be quicker than what I am to catch a gentleman of the road. Cost you much, sir? And I hope as how Master Max is all right.' And he gave Prince a pat and climbed back on to his perch. 'It's a good job we don't meet many of their sort, if you asks me.'

44

George shrugged his shoulders, followed Max back into the carriage and they were on their way back to Halstock once again, albeit at a much steadier pace from the sobered Samuel.

Maxine herself found that she was thrilled rather than scared by the encounter and had forgotten the altercation that had been about to take place when the highwayman had stopped the carriage.

It came as rather a shock when, settled once again in her corner, she found her cousin George regarding her with a leer – it was the only word she could think of to describe his changed expression.

Gone was the torpor and haze of the day's drinking and gambling and she thought he looked as though he had discovered treasure. She braced herself for an argument and possibly a scuffle.

'You did well, Max, damme if you didn't. I'm proud of you. I think the time has come.'

Fearlessly she looked into lusting eyes. 'Time for what, Cousin?' she asked in a clear tone, knowing very well what he meant.

'Time for you to have done with breeches and jackets and for me to buy you some stylish dresses with a fashionable low neck to show off what I know lies beneath the waistcoat. In fact, time to become my wife, Maxine.'

Maxine kept her temper. 'I find you loathsome, Cousin. I am of no mind to marry anyone until at least I have got the thatch for the two farmhouses.'

He slid nearer to her but did not touch her. 'Have I heard you correctly, Maxine? I talk about a cosy life as my wife and you talk about thatch? What has that to do with the matter?'

'Everything. I have promised myself that I will remain your steward until I have got the Grattans and the Lockyers under a dry roof. The cottages need new thatch. That is what I am talking about.' Maxine knew that she sounded haughty but did not care.

'Gammon. You have no idea what thatch would cost and I will need the money for your gowns and dresses.' He moved closer, his arm around her shoulder.

She stiffened but did not move an inch. 'I do know what thatch costs, I have been into it. I know to the last halfpenny how much I would need. And if you refuse to find the money then I shall get it somehow, even if I have to steal it.'

Instantly she knew she had said too much and had spoken unwisely.

He simply laughed at her and, his hands on her shoulders, pulled her roughly into his arms. 'You amuse me, Maxine, dammit if it won't be fun being married to you. Thatch indeed. Give me a kiss, and we'll go to the mantua-maker, get you kitted out in style and announce our betrothal.'

And struggle though she might, his lips were on hers and she knew nothing but disgust. She kicked out at him then and he sprang apart with a hearty laugh. 'Little spitfire, what? I'll enjoy the taming of you, I do think I will. Coming up to two-and-twenty, are you not? We'll be wed on your birthday. I look forward to the day already. No need to wait for your fortune, it's another three years yet.'

And he sat back in his corner again, fingers pressed together, pleased with his plans, gloating at his ploy. Maxine's brain was whirling at a frightening rate and went on doing so until she got to her bedroom and was on her own at last.

Even when she was in her gentleman's nightshirt, she did not get into bed but sat in the big chair by the fire from which the embers still glowed.

She was frowning deeply, for her thoughts made no sense to her. Cousin George, the mask of the highwayman, the muddled surprise on the face of poor Samuel-coachman, the thatched roofs on the two cottages in her care, and last of all, the horror of George's lips on hers.

She sat quite still and gradually the disorder of her mind settled itself into ideas and plans. Some were plausible, some ridiculous, but at the back of them all came the words of the highwayman. She muttered them over and over again – 'if ever you want employment' – then dismissed them as balderdash and tried to think sense.

I've come to the time when I have to cease being Max; I knew it would have to come one day and the events of these last hours seem to have made it not only clear, but urgent.

I love it here in Dorset. To make Triscombe House my home would not be hard, but married to Cousin George? She gave a shudder as she remembered the kiss.

But I do so want to see the Grattans and the Lockyers decently housed. They are such good, honest and hard-working people and they have been more than kind to me. I suppose I could blackmail Cousin George into having the thatching done. I could tell him I would only marry him if he set the cottages in order. But still she shuddered. It is too big a price to pay, she decided.

And slowly the germ of an idea took hold of her feverish, seeking brain. I said I would steal but how would I go about it?

Rob the rich to help the poor? At least to provide a new roof over their heads. That is what Robin Hood did, how I used to love those old tales with my cousins. It all seemed very romantic to us. . . .

Then suddenly, vividly and urgently, she had the answer. And it came with the remembrance of a masked face at the carriage door in the twilight of that evening. It came to her with the same instinctive action of knocking the pistol from his hand, ignoring all danger. And finally it came with his fading words as he rode away. 'Lovely countryside is Dorset.'

Maxine got up from the chair and flung herself on the bed, thumping the pillows violently. 'I'll do it. I'll ride out and hold up a coach or a carriage and I'll demand money. Then I'll get the thatcher in. It is not difficult, it only needs nerve and I do not lack that. I might have to go out only twice to repair the two cottages. Then I'll confess it to Cousin George and he is sure to send me away. He would never want me for a wife with that disgrace hanging over my head.

It was hours before she fell asleep; hours in which she planned the best places to wait, the finding of a mask – though this seemed the most difficult; the pistol was no problem for her cousin had taught her to shoot. Indeed, he had taken her out shooting with him and she knew she could lay hands on the type of gun she would need.

Maxine slept for only a few hours and awoke in a fever of excitement as her startling plans and ideas came flooding back to her. The cool of the morning or the soothing power of sleep made her think more cautiously, but within the hour, her mind was made up for her when a distraught Mrs Grattan arrived in the kitchen.

'Master Max,' she cried out. Maxine had never seen the good farmer's wife at a loss or so upset before.

'What is it, Mrs Grattan? Is Mr Grattan all right, and the children?'

'They'm fine just about, sir, but do you come and see what's happened for yourself. I knew it would happen one day and it has. All that rain last night and the roof fell in. And right on top of us though we'm none of us hurt, thank the Lord. Please come, Master Max, I'm sure I don't know what we'll do unless you persuade Mr Lidiard.'

Maxine followed Mrs Grattan and found the cottage in a poor state. Mr Grattan was pulling the sodden straw matresses down the ladder and putting them as near to the meagre fire as he could.

It needed only a glance at Mrs Grattan's tears and the despair of Mr Grattan lifting the wet mattresses to make Maxine decide what to do.

'Mrs Grattan, I will send cushions for you to sleep on tonight and by tomorrow, I'll have Mr Fowles, the thatcher, here. It's a promise.'

A whisper that was desperately hopeful came as a reply. 'How will you get the money, Master Max?' asked the farmer's wife.

'Don't you worry your head about it. I have some of my mother's jewellery which I can sell. You go about your work and in a few days' time, we'll have you all in order and dry and snug. I'll see to it all, but you must trust me and not ask any questions.'

Maxine went back to Triscombe House, her mind made up and full of hope. She had lied to Mrs Grattan and was intending to break the law, but all this seemed nothing when she thought of what she was going to achieve.

That day, she drew a sketch of the turnpike road between Dorchester and Yeovil and studied it; she knew it well from her visits to the market.

Then she went over in her mind the things that were of prime importance. A good horse, both fast and steady; she had that in Remus who had replaced the faithful Liddy; an intimate knowledge of the road and where to find groups or copses of shady trees; also the escape route across the fields to Halstock.

She took two days to ride her route when she should have been about the estate. She procured a mask at Dorchester on market day, and she found the pistol she needed in the gun-room and Cousin George never knew it was missing. She even visited Mr Fowles the thatcher, so sure of her success that she asked him to start the work.

Her cousin was no more bother to her and for this she was very thankful; he seemed certain of the idea of a forthcoming marriage and went off on one of his visits to Weymouth. Maxine had long since discovered the existence of Diana Chudleigh and was grateful to the unknown charmer for the days she kept Cousin George away from Halstock.

Then she chose her evening and it was all much easier than she had expected it to be. Cousin George was in Weymouth; it was the faithful Mrs Turnbull's evening for visiting her sister in Halstock, and it was fine and dry.

She told the stable boy he could have the evening off, saddled Remus herself and set off down the narrow bridle-way which lay between Triscombe House and the turnpike road, skirting Halstock village and avoiding Lidiard Manor.

There came her first disappointment. She found her dim cover under a canopy of beeches and waited, but the road was deserted. She forced herself to wait quietly and patiently, but the waiting seemed to heighten her nerve and her sense of excitement. Will I be able to do it, she kept asking herself?

The mail coach came and went, driven fast by four splendid horses; then came a farm cart, and then another farm cart. Almost an hour had passed by and the daylight had almost faded when from her vantage point under the trees, Maxine saw the carriage. She knew her time had come.

She drew in her breath, spurred Remus into action, and gripped her pistol. Within seconds she had halted the carriage and was levelling the pistol at the gentleman who was leaning out of the window.

'I want your money,' she said, her voice deep and steady. 'None of your fancy goods, just the money.'

Then she saw with a sinking heart that there was a young child in the carriage, a small boy whose eyes were popping with excitement. 'Give him your purse, Papa. It is a highwayman. A real one.'

The man gave a glance back at the boy and then turned to Maxine. 'I want no trouble,' he said. 'Put your pistol away. You can take my purse and Robert here can boast of the day he was held up by a gentleman of the road, though you look more like a gentleman than of the road, I must say. Here, take it.'

Her pistol slipped into her pocket, Maxine took the purse, muttered 'Thank you, sir,' turned Remus and rode from the scene. She heard the carriage go on its way and stopped breathless under the trees. She found that she was very hot, her eyes threatened to shed tears and she was still clutching the purse. It can't be as easy as that, she was saying to herself as she headed Remus across the fields for home. Perhaps there is nothing very much in the purse though it feels heavy enough.

Within a very short time, she had rubbed Remus down and was climbing the stairs to her bedroom. She felt strangely subdued. That was until she emptied the contents of the purse on to her bed and the guineas and the sovereigns lay glinting on the quilt.

It's enough to do Downs Farm and some over for The Elms, she was thinking. I feel guilty but I must try not to. He was a very wealthy-looking gentleman and would probably be pleased if he knew that his money was giving comfort to some poor cottager. Not all gentlemen are like my cousin George.

The weather was set fair that week and George Lidiard was still away in Weymouth. Maxine set Mr Fowles to work and planned the next night's escapade. It would not be so easy as Mrs Turnbull was there, but Maxine made the excuse of an evening visit to Lidiard Manor.

That night, Maxine had no wait and could not believe her luck; a slow horse and a grand carriage this time, and an elderly gentleman on his own. He threw her his purse without a word, grumbling that the roads were not safe these days and it seemed to be wise to take a spare purse in case of a hold-up.

When she got home, Maxine wondered if he had thrown her his real purse in mistake for his 'spare' one. It held as many coins as she had collected the night before. She sat down on her bed and wept as she realized she had done what she had planned to do in two easy excursions against the law.

It cannot be as simple as that, she told herself. Why is it? And she sat and thought that it must be because there were so many poor people that many of them became highwaymen as an easy way of providing for their families. She had the feeling that it was worse in places like London, where on Hounslow Heath was to be found violence and shooting. Her dear quiet Dorset was different, she tried to excuse herself.

Maxine's success went to her head. She had two teams of thatchers working on the cottages and she was looking at the decaying wood of the windows. Just once more, she decided, I have not harmed a soul and I have brought two poor families a good deal of comfort and happiness.

And so it was on the last night before Cousin George was due to return, that Maxine set off for her usual place under the elms. The waiting was endless and nothing passed by except two curricles and the usual mail. She had almost given up when a feeling that she could never afterwards explain, made her ride on through the village of Stratton to a dense copse of trees just outside Dorchester.

It was a good place for she could not be seen and she had a clear view along the road; she was about a mile from the turnpike and she did not wish to show herself.

Minutes before she determined to give up and go home, she heard the sound of wheels on the roughly made road and horses' hoofs in a quick and steady pace.

In the poor light, she saw the carriage come sharply round the corner drawn by a team of two horses. It was moving so quickly, she had to act before she had time to realize that the coachman had a groom up beside him. She dug her heels into Remus's side, gripped her pistol tightly and confronted the carriage. She was never able to remember exactly what happened next.

FOUR

*J*NSIDE THAT SAME carriage, on a crisp and cool evening in October, sat Sir Rupert Wootton. He was travelling to his home at Wootton Magna having spent the day doing business in Dorchester. They had gone through the turnpike and, very soon, he expected the carriage to turn from its fast pace along the turnpike road to the narrow rutted lane which led to his home at Wootton Magna Hall, halfway between Maiden Newton and Cerne Abbas.

His business had been concluded successfully and not for the first time these last three years since his wife had died, Sir Rupert wished that he was going home to a kindly and sympathetic ear. He could have remarried, but he had made up his mind that he would only marry for love and not for expediency. He was acutely aware that his two children, Gareth aged eighteen and Jessica at seventeen, needed a mother. Needed someone to care for them other than himself and his willing dab of a cousin, Elsie, whom he had brought to Wootton Magna to manage his household for him.

He knew this journey too well to want to look out at the passing countryside; in any case, it was getting dark. His thoughts back in the past, he was ill-prepared for the sudden jerking halt of the carriage and mayhem outside. Shouts of 'Fire, Jem, damn you,' from Adam, his stalwart coachman, then the unmistakable sound of the blunderbuss being fired.

Like lightning, Sir Rupert was out of the carriage to be met by a chaotic scene.

His groom holding the still smoking blunderbuss, a scared look on his face.

His coachman bending over a still figure lying in the road.

A frightened horse pawing fretfully at the ground near the fallen man.

'You've gone'n killed him, you fool,' Adam-coachman was saying. 'You was only meant to aim for his pistol. What will Sir Rupert say now—' He broke off as his master approached the group. 'It were a highwayman, sir, came up at us waving a pistol. Jem took a shot at 'un and look what's happened.'

'Be quiet,' snapped Sir Rupert bending over the still figure. 'He's not dead though a ball has gone through his sleeve. Look at this bump coming up on his forehead, obviously he knocked himself out when he fell off his horse.' Quickly, he whisked off the mask and gave a gasp of surprise. He looked at his coachman. 'He's only a young lad. Help me into the coach with him and we'll get him to Wootton Magna. You ride his horse, Jem.'

Sir Rupert had given a gasp when he had removed the man's mask for the face, so white and still, could not have been any older than his son. A handsome youth, too.

And so Maxine was lifted into Sir Rupert Wootton's carriage and the order was given to drive home carefully.

We can't have killed him, Sir Rupert was thinking furiously, and he slipped his hand under the well-fitting coat considering it strange wear for a gentleman of the road. He found the lead balls from the blunderbuss embedded in the padding of the shoulder.

'Dammit, they've not touched him,' he muttered. Quickly he undid the waistcoat and shirt to reveal a slim white shoulder and the swell of a soft female breast.

'Good god, he's a girl. What goes on?' He said the words aloud. Sir Rupert was not easily shocked but he found his heart was pounding. He looked at the face again and could see that the person he had thought was a handsome youth, if clothed in dresses and ringlets could be quite lovely. Hastily, having made sure that no injury had been sustained, he fastened the shirt and waistcoat and removed the lead balls from the jacket.

What do I do now? She is obviously disguising herself, but why play the highwayman? I think I will keep her secret and get her safely to Wootton as the young man she is pretending to be.

In the space of time it had taken him to make his startling discovery, the carriage had travelled the length of the poor lane and was bowling up the drive of Wootton Magna Hall.

The hall had been in the Wootton family for centuries and still maintained its solid, low, compact style of the reign of Elizabeth.

Maxine was carried in and Sir Rupert tried to quell the bedlam and curiosity his arrival had caused.

Jessica and Gareth were at the door and calling for their cousin Elsie.

'Papa, what is it? Have you had a duel and wounded a man? Oh, he is no more than a boy. He is very handsome lying there so still.' Jessica was almost jumping up and down in her excitement.

Their cousin Elsie arrived on the scene and Rupert thought he was going to have the added trouble of attending a swooning female.

'Oh, my goodness,' breathed the little woman. She was indeed small and plump, but although her nature was timid, she was very kind-hearted. 'Poor young man. Is he alive? Bring him into the drawing-room, I have kept the fire going for you. I will get the hartshorn. Jessica dear, don't crowd round. Please open the door for your papa and let him put the young man on the sofa. Is he badly injured?'

'He has had a fall and I think he is merely stunned,' said Sir Rupert shortly, and he carried his burden into the drawing-room with the help of Gareth.

It was by now past eight o'clock and Rupert was thinking rapidly. Whoever this is and wherever he or she came from, there would be somebody worried that he had not returned home. He looked at his two children.

'Gareth, Jessica, I want you to go to bed. I will stay with the young man. When he comes round, he will not want a set of strange faces looking at him.'

'But, Papa, do at least tell us how you came upon him.'

Rupert Wootton decided not to tell the truth. 'I think his horse must have bolted with him. We found him unconscious with his horse looking over him. I thought it best to bring him here.'

Reluctantly they left the room and Rupert's first thought was that he must now swear his coachman and his groom to secrecy in respect of the hold-up. His hand on Maxine's pulse, he looked at the still face in front of him and gave a rueful smile. I have stumbled on a mystery, he told himself, and he felt a strong pull of sympathy towards the person only he knew to be a girl.

About twenty minutes later, Maxine started to get restless. She muttered names and words, but very indistinctly and Rupert could pick out only a few. Max, she cried out, Max. Then more quietly what sounded like Cousin George and Mr Fowles. And more mysteriously – thatch. Thatch, thatch, she said it again and again.

Sir Rupert was a tall man, but not broad-shouldered; he carried his height with elegance and with his dark hair and brilliant blue eyes, his prosperous estate and his recent widowhood, he was much sought after by the husband-hunting mamas in that part of Dorset. As he sat looking at the restless figure in front of him, he knew instinctively that her eyes, when at last she opened them, would be blue.

When Maxine stopped her thrashing about and did open her eyes, memory came but slowly to her and she felt frightened. Her eyes seemed to see a fashionable carriage, her ears seemed to hear the roar of a blunderbuss, and she could still feel the blast of it on her shoulder.

Her hand went automatically to the top of her arm and finding that it did not hurt her, she looked around.

She saw nothing but eyes as blue as her own regarding her with a kindly expression from what seemed a great height. She turned her head and her mind registered an elegant drawing-room.

Back to the blue eyes and she whispered her first words. 'Where am I?'

She tried to sit up but a firm hand laid her back against the cushions; then the same hand kept hold of hers and she felt both a strength and a comfort from the stranger in front of her.

Rupert spoke slowly and firmly. 'You are at Wootton Magna Hall, near Dorchester. I am Sir Rupert Wootton. Do you remember anything?'

Memory came flooding back and Maxine shut her eyes in horror. She had been trying to hold up a coach and the groom had suddenly lifted his blunderbuss; the last thing she remembered was the loud blast and the shock which had made her fall off Remus to the ground. I must have knocked myself out, she told herself. Then with wry amusement, what a coil!

She looked again at the gentleman who sat at her side. Sir Rupert Wootton? She had a feeling that her Uncle Thomas knew a Wootton. He is not old, she thought, he seems to have a certain distinction about him.

'Were you in the carriage?' she asked timidly.

'Yes, I was. I brought you here because I had no idea who you were. You obviously have a memory of the incident, but I want no explanations now. The morning will do for that. But you must tell me one thing: is there anyone who will be anxious because you have not returned home? You do not seem to be the ordinary gentleman of the road.'

Maxine flushed. 'I must tell you—'

'No, it will wait until the morning. I want you taken to a bedroom and I want you to sleep. Do you think you could just tell me your name.'

'It is Max. Max de Rochefort.'

Another mystery, thought Rupert, a French name. I think it will turn out to be Maxine, though I will never let her know that I have discovered the secret of her sex.

'And are you staying at an inn or somewhere like that?'

'No, I live at Halstock, Triscombe House. I live with my cousin, George Lidiard, but he is not there. It is Mrs Turnbull who will be worried; she is the housekeeper. She will be expecting me back at any time for it is nearly dark. Could a message be sent to her? Just to tell her that I am safe.'

'I will send a message directly if you will promise to let my cousin Elsie – she is my housekeeper, I have no wife – show you to the guest bedroom. I will ask her to find one of Gareth's nightshirts for you. Gareth is my son; he is very much your height and build.'

By now, Maxine had fully regained her senses and was frightened of the consequences of the evening's foolhardy behaviour.

'Will I be left on my own?' she asked clearly. 'I am still feeling a little hazy about things.'

'Yes, of course. I will tell both the children not to worry you until we have had a talk in the morning. Now I will go and ask Jem – the groom who shot at you with the blunderbuss – to ride over to Halstock himself.'

'Thank you, Sir Rupert,' said Maxine and stood up. But she was more wobbly than she had realized and was glad of the steady hand of her host. They looked at one another, each with their own thoughts. Here is a man I could respect, Maxine said to herself, it would be a different story if it was he who wanted to marry me and not my cousin. But he will only ever know me as the young highwayman who held him up on the Dorchester road. And she felt sad.

And Rupert had similar thoughts. Here is a young womann I could admire and love, but what chance is there when we have met in such peculiar circumstances. She must never find out that I know her to be a girl.

Cousin Elsie came and was all concern for the young man whom she escorted up to a small bedroom; then she sent for warm water and a nightshirt.

Maxine said nothing except to thank the little lady, then she was glad of a hasty wash. She was half afraid to take off her breeches and coat and put on the nightshirt, but she did so quickly and settled down in the bed thinking that she would never sleep a wink. As it happened, she fell immediately into a deep sleep from which she did not stir the whole night.

In the meantime, Sir Rupert had sought out Adam-coachman and the groom.

He told them briefly who the young man was. 'I want to make it clear that I want not a word said about the events of the evening. You will have guessed that this was no ordinary high-wayman. I believe it to have been a prank which was done as a wager or some such thing. So, no gossip from either of you, if you please, or you will find youselves with no employment and no references. I would not like that to happen as I value the services of you both, even if Jem is not an expert with the blunderbuss . . . perhaps it is just as well.'

He saw them grin at each other and knew that he could be certain of their loyalty. 'Here is a note, Jem. Please take it to Triscombe House; it is on the edge of Halstock. The moon is rising so you will not find the going difficult.'

Rupert walked back to the Hall feeling satisfied. It is no use speculating, he was thinking. I must put the charming young lady out of my thoughts until I hear what she has to say for herself in the morning.

Maxine woke early; it was barely light. At first she was confused, but the throbbing lump on her forehead brought back a clear memory of what she had done.

I am a fool, she told herself. I need not have gone out last night; I already had enough money to mend the cottage roofs. I was deceived by my success into thinking that highway robbery was an easy game. Sir Rupert Wootton? He seemed kindly enough and he brought me here, but will he turn me over to the magistrate? I have committed a crime and I should have remembered the fates of Claude Duval and Dick Turpin early last century. They were both hanged for their crimes. And she gave a shudder.

Then, thrusting these disturbing thoughts to one side, she leapt out of bed and started to dress. She found the scorched holes in the shoulder pad of her coat and gave a thankful sigh that she had not been hit. Sir Rupert would surely have found out her identity and the game would be up.

Dressed in her own clothes once again, she felt confident and ready to meet her rescuer. Her confidence was shattered three minutes later when she found the staircase and made her way downstairs; she could hear young voices coming from what she thought must be the breakfast-room. So I am not up first; I seem to remember Sir Rupert's son and daughter. She told herself that she must think of a tale that would convince them of the circumstances of her having been brought injured to Wootton Magna. There, I've remembered the name, she thought rather proudly.

A second later, she became dizzy, lost her footing and fell down the last three steps into the large entrance of Wootton Magna Hall.

Before she had time to get herself up, Jessica and Gareth were at her side and helping her to her feet.

'I am sorry,' she said, trying to remain composed. 'I suddenly became dizzy. It must be something to do with the bump on my head, I must look as though I've been in a prize fight.'

Gareth held on to her arm and led her into the breakfast-room. Jessica – looking very pretty in a dress of blue printed cotton which suited both her fair curls and the autumnal chill – showed kindness and concern.

'You should not have got out of bed. Papa is sure to be cross with you. May we call you Max? He told us your name and you seem to be the same age as we are. I am Jessica and I am seventeen, and my brother is Gareth and he is nearly nineteen. . . .'

'Don't prose on so, Jessie,' interrupted her brother, as he helped Maxine into a chair at the breakfast-table. 'Yes, I am Gareth. Jessica will pour you some coffee and you will feel better. Will you have some toast, or have you no appetite?'

Maxine looked at the young man gratefully. Gareth Wootton was as dark-haired as his father; Jessica must take after her mother, thought Maxine irrelevantly. Then she pulled herself together thinking that coffee and toast was a good idea.

In a few minutes, she began to feel better and fit enough to answer the questions with which the two young Woottons bombarded her.

'How did you come to have that dreadful bump on your head? We thought that you and Papa must have been in a fight.' This was from Jessica.

I must be careful what I say, thought Maxine, I don't know how much their father has told them. But they proved to be so open and friendly that her task was made easy.

'Papa said you had fallen from your horse, but it must have been more than that because you have holes in your coat at the shoulder as though someone has shot at you,' said Jessica.

Maxine's mind worked feverishly. A half truth, she decided, would do. 'It all happened so quickly. Your papa was very kind. I was returning from a visit to Dorchester – I had stayed later than I had meant to do – to my home in Halstock. You may know it. There seemed to be a hold-up just past the turnpike. Remus, he is my horse, took a fright and reared up. Stupidly, I couldn't hold on and came off with a bump. Then I heard shooting, but I didn't think I'd got caught in it until your father showed me my jacket ... look, you can see the holes, they are not very big. I had been knocked out when I fell and he brought me here and you know the rest-. . . .'

'You sound as though you have got over your fall, young man.' They all turned as they heard a voice from the doorway.

Sir Rupert stood there, tall and slender yet imposing in impeccable buff breeches and boots; his coat was a navy that was almost black and his waistcoat a very pale cream. He had a quizzical expression and Maxine guessed that he had been standing there while the story was told and knew that it was less than the truth.

He joined them at the breakfast-table.

'Max fell down the stairs,' said Jessica.

Rupert looked at Maxine, a slight line of worry on his forehead. 'What is all this?' he asked gently.

Maxine smiled at him. He was all she remembered him to be. 'It was nothing. As I reached the bottom of the staircase, I felt very dizzy and I fell. You will see that I have come to no harm. Jessica and Gareth were soon there to help me up and insisted that I eat some breakfast.'

'I think we will have our good Dr Mayhew in to ask his opinion,' Rupert stated rather firmly.

Maxine felt alarmed and spoke hastily. 'No, no, there is no need at all. I will be fit enough to ride back to Halstock this afternoon.'

Rupert looked at her and knew immediately the cause for her alarm. He tried to reassure her. 'He can have a look at that bump on your head to tell you if you need to rest for a while.' He had eaten nothing but had finished his coffee and now rose and put out a hand towards her. 'Come along to the library and we will have a chat. I have a feeling that I am known to the Lidiard family.'

Maxine experienced a sense of apprehension and alarm, wondering if these were going to be her last moments as Max de Rochefort. And if, by the end of the day, she would be standing before the magistrate.

The library was small and well lined with books, but there was a handsome brick fireplace in which the logs burned cheerfully. She expected to face Sir Rupert across his desk, but he directed her into a fireside chair and sat opposite her.

'You have a lot of explaining to do, but first you will tell me about the dizzy spell that overcame you. Are you fit to answer my questions?' He was serious and calm and did not seek to intimidate her.

'It was nothing. I am quite well now, though I have to admit to a throbbing head, no more.' Maxine could not stop herself from asking with an urgency the question which most occupied her mind. 'Are you going to turn me over to the magistrate, Sir Rupert?'

Their eyes met across the fireplace, hers fearless, and his thoughtful yet searching. 'Do you think I should?' he asked bluntly.

Maxine did not falter. 'I know that what I did was against the law even though I did not rob you. I think it is a crime in itself to hold someone up at pistol point.'

He continued to regard her thoughtfully. 'I am glad that you are aware of your misdemeanour, but I find your behaviour puzzling. It is quite obvious that you are a gentleman and have no need for the proceeds of armed robbery. Did you do it as a dare? Or simply a prank? I think you had better tell me the truth and not the trumped-up tale that I heard you giving to my children.' He paused. 'I think somehow that it would be wise to stick to that story. As it happens, it bears out what I have told Adam-coachman and the groom who shot you last night. No one will know the real truth except yourself.'

'That is kind of you, Sir Rupert. Why are you saying that? I do not deserve it, you know.' Maxine was wondering if she was to escape punishment after all.

Sir Rupert gave a small smile of amusement. 'I hardly know myself; perhaps I will be able to tell you one day. It rather depends on the explanations you are going to give me. Tell me about yourself. You are a Lidiard?'

Maxine drew a deep breath. 'My mother was a Lidiard and I live at Triscombe House in Halstock with my cousin, George Lidiard. My uncle who is the sixth earl lives at Lidiard Manor.'

'He is known to me; we have occasionally met on the hunting field, but I think it is his son I know the better.'

Maxine nodded. 'Yes, he is my cousin Thomas. He is the heir and lives at Lidiard Manor with his children. They are my age and I was educated with them.'

Rupert nodded, he was putting odd pieces of local knowledge together and he had the feeling that something was beginning to make sense. 'And your mother?'

He was not prepared for the sudden crumbling in the expression on Max de Rochefort's face. 'I am sorry, do I ask something difficult?'

'It is all so long ago . . . I always remember it with sadness, but it seems to affect me more this morning. My mother would have been ashamed of me, I think, yet in a way I think she might have done just the same.'

'Would you rather not talk about it?' he asked.

'No, it is quite simple. My mother married the Comte de Rochefort and my grandmama Lidiard disapproved. We lived in Paris. I cannot recall a time when there was not trouble, though I was too young to remember the storming of the Bastille when the Revolution started. We feared for our lives after that, but Papa was spared . . . that was until Robespierre came to power . . . I cannot speak of it.'

Rupert put out a hand. 'Please, Max, I had not meant to probe into your life and to upset you. Tell me how you came to England.'

'I would like you to know the truth and then you will see how I had the need to play the highwayman.'

Rupert was still puzzled. Her words explained the flight to England, but why pose as a young man? 'Very well, as long as it not too difficult for you.'

'It was in 1794; Mama and Papa were taken to the guillotine and my br— sister with them. I escaped with our old gardener and then Cousin George came to bring us to England. Grandmama had sent him for us all to go, but it was too late.' Maxine paused and he could see her thoughts flicking over the failed to notice her hesitation over the mention of her brother. 'Cousin George gave me a home and I had my cousins. Then when I was old enough, I became his steward and I am still his steward.'

There was a long silence as she finished speaking.

Rupert felt alarm, for George Lidiard's ways were known throughout the county. But even this knowledge did not explain the highwayman prank.

'George Lidiard is your cousin?'

'Yes; he gave me a home,' she replied quietly.

'He is reputed to be mean-fisted.' Rupert said the words deliberately.

'He has money enough for some things,' Maxine said drily.

'But not for his estate?'

Their eyes clashed. 'How did you know?' she asked him.

'Maybe it is rumour, but I think he spends more money at the gaming table at Weymouth than he does on his tenants' cottages.'

'You know about it.' He could hear a world of relief in her words.

'Tell me,' he said briefly, and knew he had come to the truth at last.

'He has good tenants, the Grattans and the Lockyers, but he will not repair their cottages. They are a disgrace to the name of Dorset landowners. The rain pours in through the thatch and the Grattans can no longer live in the upstairs room. Cousin George would not let me have the money to repair the roof and I quarrelled with him. I said I would get the money somehow even if I had to steal it.'

She has courage and it explains the thatch, Rupert thought. 'So you turned highwayman?'

'Yes, why not?' she replied defiantly.

'A nineteenth-century Robin Hood, you mean.' He was

almost teasing her when he should have been chiding; most things were clear to him now.

'Oh, you do understand, thank you. Sir Rupert, I went out only twice. It was easy. I could not believe how easy it was. I hurt nobody and in two nights, I had enough money to give to Mr Fowles, the thatcher. He and his men will be working even now. When I reach home, the work will be done. I am going to tell George I still had Mama's diamond ring and that I sold it in Dorchester.'

'You tell lies very easily, Max.' Rupert knew why but he wanted to hear what she would say.

Maxine was defiant. 'There are times in life when it is necessary to lie and if the end is good, I do not see that it is wrong.'

'You have an odd idea of the truth,' he said drily. 'Are you trying to justify your highwayman act?'

'No, it was wrong, I do know that. But I believe there is an old saying "the end justifies the means".'

Rupert laughed then. 'That is very debatable, Max. But as no harm has come of your attempts to take the law into your own hands, I will not argue with you. Your farmers have their thatch, you are unharmed and it has brought you to Wootton Magna.'

She looked at him in astonishment. 'But you make it sound as though you are pleased that I am here.'

Rupert was not going to admit to his own feelings on the matter even to himself, but he was honest with Maxine.

'Perhaps you will enliven our lives for a short while. I have a feeling that Dr Mayhew will make you stay quiet until that bump on your head has gone down and your dizzy spells are over. What shall we do about your cousin George?'

Maxine's reply was instant. 'I think we might send him back to his mistress in Weymouth.'

'Max!'

'Sir Rupert,' she replied. 'I am no young innocent. I am two-and-twenty, you know.'

He looked at her: the long intelligent face, the fine eyes, yes, she did look older than the youth he had thought her to be. 'That puts us fifteen years apart, not so very much after all.'

'Does it matter?' she questioned him, not understanding his remark.

'I don't know, it might do,' he replied.

'Now you are being enigmatic, Sir Rupert.'

'I think you might call me Rupert if you are two-and-twenty.' He amazed himself at his own words; there were surprises at every turn with this young guest of his.

'I think I will stick to the "sir", it sounds more respectful,' she said quickly.

'You mean you are a respectful highwayman? We have not discussed that at length, I still have decisions to make about you, but I think I hear a carriage on the drive. That will be Dr Mayhew.'

The story of Maxine's fall from her horse was told to the good doctor who declared exactly what Sir Rupert had foretold. Stay quiet for three days, no wine or spirits, perhaps a little small ale. And no riding for a week when he would call again and would expect to find the young man a lot better. Be prepared to stay at Wootton Magna for two weeks if Sir Rupert would permit it. Oh, and short walks in the garden would be allowed if it was fine and warm.

Gareth and Jessica had known Dr Mayhew all their lives and saw him off with pleasure, glad to have their intriguing visitor to themselves. And Jessica more than happy to have a handsome young man who was not a brother in the house.

But Sir Rupert still had matters to settle with his unexpected guest and would not let her join his children until he had talked to her again.

'It is a fine morning, Max, I think Dr Mayhew would permit you to walk as far as the summer-house with me. We can be private there.'

FIVE

THE GARDENS OF Wootton Magna Hall were still formally laid
out with many features of an Elizabethan garden. Maxine
had never seen a knot garden before and was fascinated by its
intricate pattern of clipped box hedge. She could have stayed there
a long time studying it, but already her legs were feeling weak
and strange and she was glad to follow Sir Rupert into the
small summer-house which was built in the same red brick as the
house.

Inside there was not much more room than for two black
wrought-iron chairs, though these had cushions on them and she
found them not uncomfortable. In fact, by the time she reached
them, she was glad to sit down.

'Still dizzy?' asked Sir Rupert as he took a seat beside her.

She shook her head. 'No, but my legs don't seem to be my own.
They are happier sitting down than standing up!' She looked
across at Sir Rupert who was regarding her with concern. At the
kind look in his eyes, the careless grace of his posture, she felt her
heart stir and was alarmed. Maxine de Rochefort, she told herself
firmly, you are in no position to start falling in love with any
gentleman. You have kept up this pretence and you must behave

as a young man not a simpering miss. 'Have you decided my fate?' she asked him.

'Tell me more about your cousin,' he directed.

Inwardly, Maxine groaned. It is the very thing I cannot do, she thought, there is no one I can tell the whole truth. Cousin George wishes to marry me and the thought disgusts me. I have to maintain my male identity for as long as I am able, and I have a feeling that it is not going to be easy here at Wootton Magna; Sir Rupert will not be readily duped. I will have to match the young Gareth in ideas and strength, and I already have the uncomfortable feeling that young Jessica will fall in love with me. But she had to answer Sir Rupert.

'Cousin George has been kind to me, especially so in offering me a home when I had lost my own in France.'

'You do not wish to fight the French? You must consider them as an enemy.' Rupert asked the question rather wickedly, intrigued to know how she would wriggle out of it.

But nothing was to daunt Maxine. 'There has been no question of it. When my cousin's steward died, I took his place. I have been his steward these five years.'

'George Lidiard could have found another steward.'

'You do not know my cousin, sir. You have learned of his reputation for being mean-fisted, but you have no idea of the whole. With me as his steward it has saved him a wage.' Maxine knew that she sounded convincing.

'And what if you wish to marry?' Sir Rupert held his breath as he waited for her reply.

It came instantly and calmly. 'It would be no problem. I would continue as steward and take my wife to live in the steward's cottage which I have kept in good order in case the occasion should arise.'

Little liar, thought Sir Rupert and so ready with her reply. I could almost hug her; I am enjoying this. 'I doubt your intended wife would approve of you playing the highwayman however "just" the cause.'

Maxine knew that the time had come to learn her fate. 'You intend to turn me over, sir?'

'I have not made up my mind. It would horrify me if your escapade should reach the ears of my son and he thought that I condoned it.' Sir Rupert leaned forward. 'Tell me why it is that you think that "the end justifies the means".'

Maxine did not reply immediately. She knew in her heart that it was wrong to turn robber, but she could see Mrs Grattan's face so clearly; she could almost feel the tears.

'I will try and explain. First of all, I do know that it was wrong. But then there are two things to consider. First of all, the money I was given at each hold-up was handed over so easily, without a thought. It meant nothing to its owner. Indeed, the second gentleman in the grand carriage kept a spare purse in case of highway robbery. The contents of that purse were enough to put a new roof on a cottage, yet the gentleman who had thrown it to me did not miss a penny of it.'

'And the second thing?'

'You will think I am sentimental, Sir Rupert,' she said before replying.

'I am the judge of that.'

'Mrs Grattan at The Elms is the kindest and most caring woman in the world. She works so hard to keep her cottage clean, to keep her children from wearing rags. And she produces the finest butter in the whole of Dorchester market. I had pleaded with Cousin George to repair the thatch but he laughed at me. He laughed at me, Sir Rupert, saying that he had better ways of spending his money. Then the morning came – goodness gracious, it is barely a week since – when I found Mrs Grattan in despairing tears. It had rained heavily in the night, the roof had fallen in and they all had to sleep on the floor downstairs.'

Maxine paused and looked at Sir Rupert. He was paying close attention and could see the humanity and sincerity in her eyes. 'You must realize, sir, that my cousin's farm cottages have no bedroom. The family climbs a ladder out of the kitchen and they sleep on straw mattresses in the roof space. Now, even the mattresses were sodden; brave, cheerful Mrs Grattan was in tears. You might think that I was just a callous youth holding up carriages on the high toby, but those tears went to my heart. I do have a heart, sir. Cousin George refused me again and I knew without any hesitation or conscience that there was only one thing I could do.'

'And that was highway robbery?' he interrupted.

She nodded slowly. 'It so happened that Cousin George and I had been held up a few nights before by a jolly fellow who just wanted a couple of sovereigns for a meal and a lodging and the rest to take home to his family. And I decided there and then that I would do the same. Rob the rich to feed the poor just like Robin Hood. People should not be kept in poverty like that when there is enough money to help them.'

She looked at him dubiously, he was so silent. 'Perhaps you are laughing at me, perhaps you think I am wicked but I would do it again if I had to. When I think now that there is new thatch going up on Mrs Grattan's roof, I cannot think it was wrong. So there you are, turn me over to the magisttrate if you so wish, I would suffer gladly for people like Mrs Grattan. Maybe it lies in my experiences in France, I don't know, for I was very young. I lost all my family then; what have I to live for if I cannot help the oppressed in this country? You may call me a revolutionary if you like.'

This last was said on a lighter note and Sir Rupert was thinking hard. How could he condemn her? This wonderful, brave girl who had catapulted so suddenly into his life. He leaned forward and felt an urge to take her hands in his. He must be careful.

'Max de Rochefort, you may be a child of the Revolution but who am I to condemn you? You could have been killed in this mad exploit of yours, yet you risked all to help the unfortunate. Can I say that is wrong? Who am I to judge? All I will say say is that it was wrong to hold up a carriage on the "high toby" as you put it. But as only good has come of your actions, I think they must remain a secret between you and me. Adam-coachman and Jem are the only ones to know some of the truth and I have made them swear to keep last night's fiasco to themselves. They won't betray me, they value their places too much. No, I won't turn you over to the magistrate. I know it is my duty to do so and I also know that it would probably mean deportation for you ... had you thought of that?'

'Yes,' she said hoarsely.

'So I am going to be as wicked as you have been and defy the law. But you must promise me never to do such a thing again.'

Maxine smiled then and Sir Rupert Wootton received a shock. It was the first time he had seen her face with a smile and as he met her eyes, he could see a radiance that betrayed her sex. She is a beauty, he said to himself, but I am the only one to know the truth. I hope that the others will think of her just as an Adonis of a young man.

Maxine felt like throwing her arms round the neck of this kind gentleman, but restrained herself rigidly and tried not to appear too excited by his verdict.

'Sir Rupert, I must thank you. You have shown nothing but kindness and I do not know how I shall ever repay you.'

He smiled, too. 'There is no need to talk of repayment. Just spend a week or two here with us at Wootton Magna and I think my children will gain from your company. It will do them good to hear of your work as steward to your cousin. I think I must spoil them because they have no mother.' He stopped and looked across at Maxine. 'My wife died three years ago.'

'You have not remarried,' she stated hesitantly.

'I have never met anyone to equal her,' he replied and found himself continuing silently, not until now.

'I expect you will one day; you cannot stay a widower all your life.' With her main anxiety settled for her, Maxine became cheerful. 'Are you a good landlord, Sir Rupert?'

'Yes, I would like to think so. Wootton Magna is a large estate. I have five farms and there is a lot of woodland. I am glad to say that I have an excellent steward whom you are sure to meet. I often ride round with him myself to make sure the farm buildings are in order.' He looked at her interested face and saw the intelligence as well as the charm. 'Now, young man, we have to decide what to do with you. If you are to stay here, you will need more clothes. You could borrow from Gareth, of course, but I think it would be better if I went over to Halstock to explain things to your cousin. We are not quite in the same part of Dorset, but it is no great distance. Do you give me your permission and shall I bring some clothes back with me?'

Maxine gave a little frown. 'I am not sure what kind of reception you will get from Cousin George. He is not going to be very pleased if I am not there to collect the rents and do the accounts.'

'Could he not do it himself?'

'He has never done so yet.' Maxine gave a wry smile. 'Mrs Turnbull will pack some of my clothes for me. I had better write and tell her to include some pantaloons and my Hessians if I am to remain here for a while. I would not like to put you to shame.'

He smiled generously. 'I don't think you will ever do that. You and Gareth are going to rival each other for good looks. You will have Jessica falling in love with you!'

He was sure he saw a slight flush on her face but she remained collected.

'I think Jessica is of an age to imagine herself in love with any young gentleman,' she said easily. 'Is it her come-out season this year?'

'No, I think she is still too young, though we may spend a little time in my London house later in the season. Does your cousin have a house in town?'

'There is Lidiard House which he shares with his cousin, Thomas. And Grandmama goes up occasionally though she prefers her quiet life at Nether Compton. She is quite elderly, you know.'

'So I believe, though I have never met her. She is reputed to be a remarkable woman. Did she receive you gracefuly?' he asked, wondering if the dowager knew that her grandson was in fact her granddaughter.

'Yes, she has been very kind. She wrote to forgive Mama for marrying a French count, but, of course, her letter arrived too late. I think she is grieved by it, but I believe her to be glad that I have come into Dorset.'

'I think I am glad, too,' he said without thinking, realized his mistake and tried to cover it up. 'I hope this will be the start of a firm friendship between you and Gareth and Jessica. I see you as a good influence on them.'

She gave a laugh. 'Even after all my iniquities? You are flattering, Sir Rupert; I am at a loss to understand why.' Maxine looked him full in the eyes; a current of feeling passed between them and she hastily dropped her glance.

He gave a short chuckle to try and pass off the tense moment. 'I might not approve of your highway capers, but I admire the way you have cared for your tenants, young man. And now I will take you back to Gareth and Jessica and you must promise to pass the days quietly. I will set off immmediately for Halstock, but do write a list for me to give to your Mrs Turnbull if there is anything in particular you wish to be sent.'

Sir Rupert Wootton travelled to Triscombe House in his curricle; he was along the turnpike road and through the village of Halstock in what seemed like no time at all. Yet he had never been on visiting terms with the Lidiards and he concluded that it must be because Wootton Magna was nearer to Maiden Newton which was where most of his friends were situated.

He had to pass Lidiard Manor and considered it to be a very substantial dwelling not unlike his own home at Wootton Magna, set in fine rolling parkland. By this time, he was hoping that he would find George Lidiard at home and when he at last reached Triscombe House, he gave a sigh of relief when he saw a carriage being led round to the stables. The timing might not be opportune, he decided, but at least my journey is not wasted.

He was let into the house by the maid, and the woman he assumed to be Mrs Turnbull appeared straight away. He smiled as he announced himself.

'Oh, Sir Rupert, what a shock I had when I received your note last night and me that worried because Master Max had not returned. The master has just this minute arrived back from his trip to Weymouth. He is quite put out, not to say anxious. Come into the drawing-room and I will bring some wine and tell Mr George that you are here.'

In the drawing-room, Rupert looked around him. Clean and comfortable, with furniture which looked as though it had seen better days, and drapes at the windows which were in need of replacement. No money spent here either, he thought grimly, and waited with curiosity for Mr George Lidiard to show himself.

He heard the voice before he saw the man and it sounded petulant.

'He has not brought Max over with him? I shall want to know why.'

Minutes later, Rupert was making his bow to a tall figure of a man who could only be described as portly. He looked to be near his fifties in age, but was dressed in ridiculously bright colours of a younger dandy; neither his cream pantaloons nor the glittering yellow waistcoat flattered him. Sir Rupert was instantly given a bad impression of Max's cousin.

'I think we know some Woottons,' George Lidiard was saying. 'Now tell me how the devil young Max came to be Maiden Newton way. And why haven't you brought him home, there are the rents to collect tomorrow? Not ill is he? Never had a day's illness in his life, very strong young man, my cousin.'

I am going to have to try to keep my patience, thought Rupert, I do not usually take a person in immediate dislike.

'I believe Max was returning from a commission in Dorchester. His horse threw him, and when I came along, he was lying unconscious in the road. As I had no idea who he was, I took him to my home near Maiden Newton.'

'Silly young jackanapes. I cannot believe that Remus threw him, Max has had him these five years. Quiet beast, very faithful.'

'I believe there was a hold-up of some kind – getting very common in Dorset it seems – shots were fired and the horse was frightened.'

'You are right,' replied George. 'Max and I got held up only the other night by some highwayman wanting a couple of guineas for a board and lodging. Don't know what it's coming to, ought to be hanged.'

Rupert looked at him curiously. 'You would hang a highwayman even though he only wanted a guinea for a night's lodging? And no one was hurt.'

George Lidiard blustered and Rupert liked him less and less. 'All deserve it, hanging's too good for them.'

'And what if the money was for his family or someone in distressed circumstances?' Rupert asked quietly.

'Balderdash. You will be talking about Robin Hood next, nothing short of a common robber. Hang them or deport them, that's what I say. Now what's all this about young Max, why have you not brought him home? Not all up with him, is it? Can't do without him, you know, best steward I ever had. I don't want my plans spoiled.'

By now Rupert Wootton was looking at George Lidiard with dislike. What plans? Cousin George must know Max to be a girl, did he have designs on her? Had this gross fellow in front of him got the most out of his young cousin and now that she promised to be a beauty, did he plan to make her his wife? Not if I have anything to say in the matter, Rupert was thinking, and yet it is nothing to do with me. I must hope that this is all show; he did after all give the young girl from France a home. Go carefully, he told himself.

'No, Lidiard, no harm done at all. Just knocked himself unconscious when he fell from the horse. Getting a bit of dizziness so I called our doctor in, but there's no call for alarm. Just to stay quiet for a week or two, Dr Mayhew said, so with your permission, I will keep him at Wootton Magna and he will be good company for my two. Gareth and Jessica seemed to be pleased with their unexpected visitor and they are of similar ages. So I have come to collect some clothes, if you will agree. Max has made a list for Mrs Turnbull.'

George Lidiard looked put out. 'Sounds as though you have put pressure on him to stay when he knows he has his duties here. However, the harvest is in and it is a quiet time of the year. The rents will have to wait. Fortunately I am having a run of luck in

Weymouth so the best thing I can do is to get myself back there. Nice little house in Weymouth, y'know, nice company, too.'

I think I must go before I lose my temper, said Rupert to himself, but he managed to maintain ten minutes of small talk while Mrs Turnbull packed a small trunk for Max. As she handed it over, she looked pleased. 'Tell him I said to rest proper,' she said. 'A couple of weeks' quiet will do him good. He works too hard here for my liking. But that's between you and me, sir.'

Rupert bade her goodbye and the trunk was put in the curricle. Standing at the front of the house with George Lidiard, he could see a farmhouse not so far away and there were men on the roof. Ha, he thought, and wondered what this Cousin George would say about it.

'You having trouble with one of your farmhouses?' he asked smoothly. 'Always something needs doing, don't you think?'

George Lidiard nodded. 'You are right. I am having to put new thatch on The Elms; costing me a fortune, but it has to be done.'

Rupert felt like knocking him to the ground. Instead he made hasty farewells, jumped up into his curricle and drove back to Wootton Magna at a furious and dangerous pace, such was his anger.

He arrived at Wootton Magna Hall to find Max, Gareth and Jessica engaged in a hilarious game of spillikins and up in the old nursery of all places. They did not even hear him open the door and he stayed still, looking at their happy faces.

'What's all this?' he said in a better humour than he had felt after leaving Max's cousin. 'I thought Max was supposed to be resting quietly.'

Jessica spoke for them all. 'Oh, Papa, we did mean to be quiet. We were showing Max over the Hall and we came to the nursery. Did you know he was brought up in France and they did not play spillikins or even Speculation. But he learned how to play with his Lidiard cousins. We were pretending we were children again.'

Rupert could not keep himself from laughing in spite of his inward rage. 'You *look* no more than children!' he said. 'But as there are four of us, we could have a rubber of whist this evening if Max feels up to it. What do you think, Max?'

Maxine was trying not to admit to herself that her heart turned over when she saw Sir Rupert at the door. It will not do, heart, she told it, please behave yourself. But she laughed with the others and said she would enjoy a game of whist though they would soon find that she was no expert.

'I have brought a trunk for you, Max,' Sir Rupert told her. 'I have had it taken to your bedroom. I hope you will find everything you need. Mrs Turnbull was most concerned and very helpful.'

'Did you see my cousin? Was he there?' she asked.

'He had just come in from Weymouth and says he will return there immediately if you are going to be here for a while. Come down to the library and I will give you his messages.'

In the library, they stood looking at each other and Maxine knew she could sense anger in Sir Rupert's expression.

'My cousin has annoyed you,' she said quietly.

'How did you know?' he asked abruptly.

'I can see it in your face.'

'You surely do not know me that well. We have not been acquainted for twenty-four hours yet.'

I feel as though I have known you all my life, she wanted to say, and once again admonished her heart and told herself she would have to be careful. 'It does not take much imagination to know that you would soon be at odds with Cousin George.'

'If it was up to your cousin, you would be hanged by now.'

She looked at him in consternation. 'You surely did not tell him?'

'No, I did not, but he did tell me of the incident that you and he had on the road and said the fellow should be hanged.'

'It is a good thing he does not know the truth,' she remarked with some feeling.

'Your secret is safe with me, Max. Do not worry. Are you usually in disagreement with your cousin?'

She nodded. 'I am afraid so.' It is a good thing that Sir Rupert does not know the whole, she thought. 'Fortunately, he is so often away at Weymouth that I am left to manage the estate on my own.'

'You will be pleased to know that the thatchers are busy on The Elms. I remarked on it to your cousin as I was leaving.'

'What did he say?' she asked curiously. 'Was he angry?'

He watched her face carefully. 'No, he said it was costing him a fortune but it had to be done.'

He waited for her outburst and then was not surprised when she almost collapsed in hearty laughter. He was getting to know her.

'Oh, if that is not just like Cousin George, he likes to be well thought of, you know.'

'And it does not vex you?'

'Oh no,' she said instantly. 'As long as I know I can keep the farmhouses warm and dry, I cannot be vexed. I know him well enough after all this time.' And as she finished speaking, a little shadow – was it of fear? he questioned – crossed her bright eyes.

She has not told me the whole, thought Sir Rupert. I wonder if the dreadful George Lidiard has designs on her virtue? I think I will take an interest in the future of the so-called Max de Rochefort.

There followed a happy time for Maxine. She was completely recovered in the week that Dr Mayhew had given her and he pronounced her to be fit and well. He told her she could ride if she wished to.

She then announced that she must go back to Triscombe House, but it took little persuasion on the part of Gareth and Jessica to make her stay longer. When Sir Rupert added his voice to theirs, she could not resist their pleas and a note was sent over to Halstock.

It was a fine autumn and the colours of the October foliage all around them made riding a pleasure. They also made an excursion to Cerne Abbas but were disappointed to find that the famous Cerne Giant to be seen on the chalk uplands, was neglected and almost overgrown with grass. The disappointment in no way diminished their enjoyment of the day's ride and a nuncheon at a local hostelry.

The following day, they were forced to stay indoors by very frequent heavy showers. Four o'clock in the afternoon found them in conversation with Sir Rupert in the drawing-room, trying to decide whether to take a late walk out.

On to this animated scene, came Cousin Elsie looking alarmed, puzzled and flustered. As though she had seen a ghost as Jessica put it afterwards.

Sir Rupert turned with a smile. 'Something has happened to upset you, Cousin, did you want me?'

Her words came in halting short sentences. 'Rupert, a young man has called ... he is ... I have put him in the library ... Rupert, he is ... oh, Rupert. . . .'

Sir Rupert got up. 'Does he wish to see me? Did he give his name?'

'His name is Rockford ... but it is not like that, Rupert, he could be a twin of Max ... please come quickly. I thought it *was* Max, I really did. You must come. . . .'

The young people had stopped talking and were listening to the confused little lady with interest.

'We will all come,' said Gareth. 'Perhaps it is a friend of Max's.'

Sir Rupert made a gesture, but it was too late to stop them. He could see that Max had a puzzled expression on her face. Then they were out of the door and on their way to the library and Sir Rupert followed them quickly.

SIX

*I*N THE LIBRARY stood a young man. He was neatly dressed in a dull grey coat and a plain waistcoat of deep fawn. He was tall but not above average and he had dark hair and brown eyes. He took a step forward as the four came into the room and then pulled himself up sharply.

Sir Rupert went forward to greet him, but the stranger's eyes went past him and fixed on Maxine who was standing as a statue in the doorway.

'You call yourself Max de Rochefort?' His voice was hoarse with emotion. 'But you cannot be for I am Max . . . you are not Max at all, you have blue eyes . . . oh, my dearest God, you must be Maxine. . . .'

There was an eerie silence as the two of them stared at each other; then Max spoke again.

'Maxine.'

Just the single word and the visitor seemed to be unable to say more.

They all heard a strangled sound from Maxine, almost a scream before she spoke in a voice that had a hysterical sound to it. 'No, no. You were taken, you died all those years ago.' She moved into the room, her eyes fixed on the person who resembled her so closely. 'Please tell me the truth. You cannot be my brother come back from the dead. Oh, please, please tell me the truth.'

The young man who called himself Rockford put his hands on her shoulders. 'Maxine, it is you. Grandmama said it was Max who was here, but I knew it could not be. Maxine, try to believe me. I did not go to the guillotine with Papa and Mama, I escaped and when I sought you out, you had gone. I have thought you dead all these years ... look, Maxine, here is Mama's ring. You must believe me.' And he took a gold ring studded with small diamonds from his little finger and gave it to her.

Maxine felt the room going round, but she managed to look at the ring she had last seen on her mother's finger. There could be no doubt.

And she threw herself into her brother's arms and sobbed uncontrollably as though all the suppressed sorrow of the years was manifesting itself in a single second.

'Max, it *is* you. Oh, Max, I cannot believe it. And look, Max.' Her fingers went up to her neckcloth and pulled at it, underneath the collar lay the silver chain and the cross. 'Mama put it round my neck as she took you away.'

He held her tightly to him, looking over the top of her head at Sir Rupert and his children who were still and staring in astonishment.

'Sir Rupert Wootton? I am sorry, sir, I had hoped to see you on your own so that I could explain myself before I saw Maxine. My grandmother told me that there was someone like me here calling himself Max de Rochefort. I could understand nothing and I wished to see you first.'

Maxine lifted her head at last; she recognized her brother's voice, she had seen her mother's ring. This was her Max come miraculously back to life. Then she remembered Sir Rupert and the young Woottons.

And she turned away from Max to find herself in the gentle, caring arms of Rupert Wootton. 'Rupert, I am sorry, you have believed me to be a young man. I have deceived you. It is true that I am Maxine de Rochefort. Will you forgive me?'

It is the first time she has called me Rupert, was his main thought as he held her close to him and stroked her dark hair. 'It is all right, little one.' I knew all the time.' Her head shot up. 'Not to worry about it now. We will leave you on your own with your brother and you can tell us the whole later. I will have some brandy sent in. Look, I will put the chairs together by the fire and you can sit near each other.'

A few minutes later, Maxine was thankful to be taking a sip of brandy and looking shyly at the person she now knew to be her brother.

He smiled at her. 'Maxine, I have given you a tremendous shock and it has been a shock to me, too. It will take me a long time to tell you the whole story. Are you quite well? Grandmama said you had been thrown by your horse.'

'It was nothing and I am quite better. Sir Rupert persuaded me to stay on here for a few days. They are very kind people and I have deceived them.'

'Oh, Maxine, I am at a loss to know where to start. Tell me your story first. To think you have been alive and posing as me all these years. It is hard to believe it. Grandmama mentioned our cousin George who was Mama's nephew. Did he give you a home? How did you get out of France? Can you bear to tell me?'

The brandy had given Maxine back her courage after her shock and she looked at Max as though she couldn't take her eyes off him. 'We are incredibly alike, are we not? You could almost take us for twins except that you are taller and you have Papa's brown eyes whereas mine are blue from Mama. Why are you laughing?'

'It was because someone told me they had seen my twin in

Dorset that I set out on my search. I remembered our grandmother lived in the county. But I will tell you all about that later,
I want to hear about you first.'

Maxine went back to the still vivid events of fifteen years
before. 'After you had gone, I stayed with Pierre. Mama had told
me to dress as a boy, yet she dressed you as a girl. I could never
understand that.'

'I think it saved our lives,' he said gently. 'Tell me about Pierre.'

'He was very good to me, but then Cousin George came with a
note from Grandmama asking us all to go to England. But it was
too late. You had all gone. Cousin George brought me to England
but he wanted me to stay as a boy. . . .'

'Why was that?'

'I will tell you later, it is too long now. I have been with him all
these years and when I finished my studies with our cousins, I
became his steward.'

'*You* became his steward? But he knew you were a young lady
. . . you do not like our cousin, I can tell.'

'I loathe him. But I will not talk about him. I have been able to
forget him while I have been here . . . oh, I don't know what
Gareth and Jessica are going to say. And Sir Rupert said he knew
I was a girl. Did he really say that? I wonder how he found out? I
must have given myself away somehow. But that is enough about
me. I want to hear about you. How did you escape the guillotine,
Max? What have you been doing all these years?'

It took the rest of the afternoon and evening for Max to tell his
sister of his life. Then after a jovial dinner with the Woottons
laughing and teasing her, Maxine went to bed but not to sleep.
Max's story went round and round in her head all night long.

On that fatal day in Paris in 1794, Max de Rochefort, aged ten
years old, obeyed his mother and put on the dress of one of the

servants over his trousers and shirt; then she gave him his father's purse to put in the pocket in the long dress. He had seen Maxine pick up the bag ready packed with one of his old suits and run out of the house to Pierre's cottage. I shall never see her again, he thought, but any sorrow or fear he felt were lost in the terrible haze of the happenings of the next hour.

Rough men, shouting curses and *Vive la Révolution* came into the house and Max and his parents were manhandled outside. His mother clutched him to her and, young though he was, he never forgot the dignity of his father. The Comte de Rochefort stood straight and still, one arm around his wife, one hand on his son's shoulder.

At the tumbril, rough hands held the boy and there was a fierce argument. Fearful though he was, Max seemed to think that the mob was disagreeing on whether a girl so young should be sent to the guillotine with her parents.

'*Maman*,' he cried out and, at the sound of his voice, he was bundled up on to the terrible cart. Then the nightmare journey. Through St Antoine, the long Rue St Honoré, the Tuileries Gardens and at last, the Place de la Révolution.

There, a stinking, heaving mass of people and Max shut his eyes. When he opened them, he saw the scaffold with its terrible instrument of death; he thought he could smell blood. He saw the rows of women there, the *tricoteuses*, they called them. He had always imagined them to have faces like witches, but he saw them sitting on their seats placidly knitting away just as a woman would in the courtyard of her home.

He buried his face in his mother's skirts and she clutched him feverishly. He heard a cry.

'Jump, *ma petite*, jump to Mère Tissot.'

'Max.' He heard the agony in his mother's voice. 'Here is my ring, take it and jump to the good woman. You are saved.'

He saw his father put out a hand towards him but the *comte* was restrained. '*Dieu te garde, mon fils*,' were the last words he heard from either of his parents.

He saw the woman standing by the now stationary tumbril which was waiting its turn and, clutching the ring, he jumped, aided by a little push from his now sobbing mother.

He felt pain in his ankle as he landed on the ground, but he was covered by the woman's black skirt and led away from the scene.

They walked a long way through narrow streets. He was limping.

'Not much further,' said his rescuer. 'You are hurt, *ma petite*? Why did you father call you *mon fils* if you are a girl? Here we are, it is small but it is clean, my home.'

Then he was inside the smallest room he had ever seen and he was made to sit on a wooden bench.

'Your name?' the woman asked. She was younger than he had first thought and her face less grim.

'Maximilian de Rochefort.'

'Then you are a boy. Why are you in a dress? I could not see a small girl go the the Razor, but what am I to do with you?'

'My mama made me dress as a girl,' he said.

'She is . . . she was wise, your mama.' She knelt and took off his shoes. 'Your ankle is very swollen; you will have to rest with me. But we will tell no one. I am not as hard as they think. You remember my name, Maximilian?'

'They call me Max, Mme Tissot,' he said quietly and forced himself not to think of the scene at the Place de la Révolution. It would be all over now and he must go home and look for Maxine.

'*Bon*, I shall call you Max, too. I will make us coffee and find a rag to bind your foot. What are you clutching?'

Max opened his fingers and saw his mother's ring.

Mme Tissot's eyes glistened. 'We could sell it for many louis,' she said.

Max jumped and then fell over as his ankle gave way with a lot of pain. 'Never,' he said. 'I will never sell it, it is all I have of Mama's. I will run away.'

'No, no, do not fear. We will manage.'

'I have some money,' he told her.

She stared. 'You have money?'

'Yes, this dress has a large pocket and Mama gave me my father's purse. I do not know how much is in it,' he replied.

'Let me see.'

Max lifted the hem of the dress and found the purse. It did not feel very heavy. 'Here you are,' he said.

Mme Tissot took the purse and opened it. 'Ten louis, *mon Dieu*. We are saved. Your papa must have meant you to jump.'

'I don't know?' Max answered miserably. 'I just want to go home.'

'And so you shall as soon as you can walk. You must keep your foot up for a few days.'

But Max was thinking of Maxine. Was she safe, too? His parents must have planned to save them. He must take care of Maxine. He was ten years old and she was only seven.

It was over a week before he could walk well enough to think about getting right across Paris. In that time, Mme Tissot was kind to him and did not go back to her knitting. He thought she did not have the hatred in her heart that was the hallmark of most of the *tricoteuses* and revolutionaries.

The day came to bid her goodbye and he said he would always remember her and he hoped that she would not get into trouble for helping the son of a *comte*.

His foot hurt him badly by the time he reached the home of the de Rocheforts. There he had a shock. The front door stood open and he hardly recognized his home; it had not been set alight, but most of the furniture was missing. Only the very biggest cabinets remained and they were empty of the family silver and the good pieces of porcelain. Even the carpet in the *salon* was missing.

He stared around him and walked slowly into the kitchen. Mme Lebecque, no servants? And Maxine? He went out to Pierre's cottage, afraid of what he might find. He knew what the plan had been. But it was deserted. No Pierre, no Maxine. Even Pierre's wooden chair was taken.

He felt tears sting his eyes then. I will not cry, he told himself. They have got Maxine and Pierre as well and now there is only me left. And he remembered what his father had told him if this dreadful thing should happen. Go to M Chardin and hide until the troubles are over and then go to M Raymond, the lawyer, and he will arrange things for you.

Max sat forlornly on the step of the gardener's cottage. My only hope is in M Chardin, he thought, Papa is right. M Chardin was his tutor; a scholarly, kindly man in his fortieth year. He had taught the de Rochefort children since Max had been four years old.

Max felt a surge of hope. I will leave this dress behind me, it has served its purpose and I can become a boy again. I'll go straight to M Chardin, he will know what to do.

The tutor lived two streets away and Max was soon with him. He found that he was expected and that M Chardin was pleased that Max had escaped but very sad about Maxine.

'Be brave, Max, your papa must be proud of you. He came to me when the Terror started and told me what to do if you came to me. I have the money and I will give you your lessons and prepare you for the university. Then you can read for the law, or for the church, whichever you prefer.

The next fifteen years went exactly as the tutor had foretold. Max, now a handsone young man, studied hard at university. But by the time he was twenty-five, he found his heart knotted with hatred for his fellow-countrymen who had put his mother and father to death.

He was out of sympathy with the Emperor Napoleon and his war with the Spanish on the Iberian Peninsula and when he learned that Sir Arthur Wellesley – later to become Duke of Wellington – had landed at Lisbon in order to fight the French, Max said goodbye to Paris and headed west into Portugal. He reached there in time to join an infantry brigade and see the enemy hustled out of Oporto.

It was to be the turning point of Maximilian de Rochefort's life, for it was here he changed his name to Max Rockford, became an Englishman – after all, he could speak the language as well as a native – and he met Freddy Courtney-Welles.

The two young men found themselves sharing a tent after the battle of Oporto and immediately formed a friendship. The light-hearted, fun-loving and fair-haired Freddy was a complete foil for the serious Max and the friendship did Max a lot of good. They were commanded to wait at Abrantes while the new plan of campaign was decided upon and to be prepared to march into Spain.

They were idle for several days before getting the orders to march and managed to exchange their life histories.

Freddy was saddened by his friend's suffering at the hands of the Revolutionaries and at the loss of his only sister.

'I have a sister,' said Freddy, as they sat under a tree trying to escape from the burning sun. 'Her name is Cecily, I call her Cecy but that is not very kind of me. She is a dear girl and can ride like the wind. She says she is only really happy when she is in the saddle and I believe her. You would like her, Max, she is fair like me. I hope to introduce you to her. Will you come back to England with me when this lot is over and Napoleon is beaten?'

Max laughed. He had not laughed so much in fifteen years as he had in the two weeks since he had met Freddy.

'You are sure we are going to win, Freddy?'

'Certain of it. Sir Arthur is better equipped in this kind of terrain. Napoleon found it easy in Italy and thinks it will be the same in Spain. But he hasn't reckoned on the lack of transport and the scarcity of provisions. Then there is this terrible heat to contend with.'

'I believe you to be right, Freddy, from the tales I have heard from the officers, but this is only the beginning.' Max was suddenly serious but Freddy soon joked him out of it.

'Have confidence, lad. With Sir Arthur as commander-in-chief we can't go wrong even in these temperatures and those mountains facing us in the distance. But getting back to England, will you come to my home in Somerset? Cecily would love to meet a hero of the Peninsula and maybe I will do a little match-making. She is supposed to marry an old family friend who is nearly twice her age and she don't like it above half.'

'How old is she?' Max asked the question with some diffidence. 'I'm not in the petticoat line, you know. I have been too busy studying all these years.'

'But you enjoy riding?'

'Oh, yes, I rode as soon as I was breeched and then when I went to live with my tutor, he insisted on providing me with a mount.'

Freddy grinned. 'There you are. You said you were five-and-twenty and Cecily is nineteen, maybe twenty by now, I forget. Couldn't be better.'

Max joined in the fun. 'We may dislike each other on sight.'

'No, you won't; I can just see the two of you together. As long as you promise to come home with me and not go back to Paris.'

'I've no intention of doing that and I will accept your invitation gladly. Maybe I will be able to seek out my grandmother if she is still alive.'

'What is her name?' asked Freddy.

'She is a Lidiard, I expect she is the dowager by now, she would be quite elderly.'

'There is a Bishops Lydeard near us in Somerset,' said Freddy promptly.

'No, it is a Dorset family,' Max relied.

'Well, they are neighbouring counties. It is all the West of England, you know.'

'Yes, I have studied the map. I would look forward to coming with you, Freddy, and to meeting Cecily, of course.'

They both laughed and the talk turned to the strategies of war.

When their march finally started, they encamped every night then set off next morning at half-past two when it was cooler.

By the 28 July, they found themselves two miles from Talavera, a small town in the wine-producing area of Spain, and battle ensued. The French were the greater in numbers, but were repulsed three times in fiercely fought skirmishes. They finally retreated across the River Alberche.

The casualties were horrendous and it was reported that the British army lost 5,000 men. Among those injured and unable to move on were both Freddy Courtney-Welles and Max himself.

They managed to stay together and found themselves stranded near the River Tagus. Max had a broken leg and Freddy, a bad wound to the eye. They had lost so many colleagues, they counted themselves fortunate.

But they were to endure many weeks in poor conditions, with supplies extremely scarce. Bread was rationed and the poor meat they received was old goat – lean and very tough.

However, they and the other wounded reached Belem just

outside Lisbon, where Max's leg was set and soothing ointments applied to Freddy's injured eye.

They stayed there for several weeks and Freddy was delighted to receive letters from his family arriving with the packet which sailed every week.

He had written to his sister and it amused him to read her reply to Max.

My dear Freddy

It was kind of you to write to me by separate mail and I hope you receive this reply before you are moved on. I am sorry to hear of the injury to your eye and must hope that your sight is not affected.

We are all pleased to hear that you will bring your friend Max home to us. I can tell you are trying your hand at match-making, but I am afraid it will be to no avail. I think you have forgot that the family wish me to marry Sir Henry Riddick, but I cannot like the idea. He is over forty years of age and seems to be as old as a grandfather to me. Besides this, he is very fat and pompous. Mama tells me that it would be an honour to be Lady Riddick of Fernleigh Hall and that it would please Papa.

Do you think your friend would elope with me? Then I would be the wife of a French count even if he has renounced his country. I have no doubt that it will amuse the two of you to plan an elopement during your idle hours in Portugal! I hope you will soon be able to sail for home.

Your affectionate sister
Cecily

The contents of this letter entertained the two young soldiers for many hours, when they hatched countless schemes to rescue Cecily from the portly Somerset gentleman.

The invalided sick all embarked for England on the 8 October and a week later, Max found himself a welcome guest at the Courtney-Welles's town house in London.

SEVEN

$\mathcal{L}$ATE OCTOBER FOUND the two young men settled in Courtney House in London, the family having removed from Somerset for the season.

Max found himself in funds as all his father's fortune and the money from the sale of the de Rochefort estate had, on the instruction of the *comte* to M Chardin, been successfully transferred by the family's Paris bank to London.

Within a week, he was able to set out with Freddy dressed in prime style and eager to visit the London clubs and coffee houses. His leg had mended, but due to the rough setting of the bone, he was left with a slight limp; he was conscious of it but managed to tell himself that he was lucky to have survived at all.

On the second week of his homecoming, Freddy left Max for a few days while he journeyed to Shaftesbury to fetch his sister, Cecily, who had been staying there with friends. While he was in Dorset and without telling Max about it, he made a point of driving a curricle down to Dorchester. His idea was to enquire into the whereabouts of Max's grandmother and any of the Lidiard family.

He learned two things which he thought would please Max. The

Dowager Countess Hampton apparently lived at Nether Compton on the border of Dorset with Somerset and her son, the sixth earl, lived at Lidiard Manor not far from Dorchester.

It was while he and Cecily were walking down the main street of Dorchester, that Freddy received a severe shock and he stood still and stared ahead.

Coming out of the main tavern in the small town and walking towards them was Max. Freddy grabbed Cecily's arm.

'Cecy, good God, there's Max, what the devil is he doing here? I left him in London.'

'It can't be, Freddy. Do you mean this dark young man walking towards us with the rather tall, burly gentleman who reminds me of Sir Henry Riddick, I'm sorry to say. . . ?'

'Max . . .' Freddy started to say as the couple passed.

The young man turned his head and in that instant, Freddy could see bright blue eyes where Max's were brown.

'Well, I'm damned,' he said. 'It was so like him that I was sure it was him. Must be his double. They say that we have all got a double somewhere in the world. I must tell Max that I saw his twin in Dorchester; he won't believe me.'

Cecily gave a laugh. 'He was very handsome,' she remarked. 'Is your Max as handsome as that?'

'Yes, I suppose you might say he is. But don't go falling in love with him, Cecy, you musn't forget Sir Henry.'

'Fiddle,' she replied. And they went on their way.

Back in London once again, the inevitable happened. The carriage dropped Cecily at the door of Courtney House and she hurried in. That afternoon, she was dressed in a dark-blue pelisse of shot silk with a white fur trim and a pale-blue bonnet. Her fair curls peeped from the bonnet and she looked enchanting. This was how Max first saw her.

He was in the drawing-room upstairs when she burst in. They stared at each other.

'It was you we saw in Dorchester,' were her first words.

'I beg your pardon?' The deep but polite voice of Max asked his question. He guessed this to be Cecily for she was expected and Freddy had described her.

'You are Max Rockford; Freddy thought he saw you in Dorchester and was going to speak to you. Then, as you got close, he could see that you had blue not brown eyes.' She stood close to him and their eyes met and held. Cecily was the first to falter under his intense gaze. 'I am sorry, I expect you think I am talking nonsense and I have not introduced myself. I am Cecily Courtney-Welles, Freddy's sister. Were you expecting me?'

He nodded. 'Yes, Miss Courtney-Welles. . . .'

'No, no, you are to call me Cecily, but not Cecy if you please. It is my naughty brother who says that and I get cross with him, though I suppose we do call him Freddy when his name is Frederick. Are you quite better now? Freddy told me that you were injured.'

Max thought he had never seen anyone so lovely. 'Yes, thank you, except for a slight limp which does not signify. And, yes, we were expecting you though Freddy omitted to tell me something,' he said.

'What was that?' She took off her pelisse and bonnet and he saw that her muslin dress was also blue and that she was slim and dainty.

'He did not tell me you were so beautiful,' Max said and surprised even himself.

Her eyes widened. 'Max – I am going to call you Max – you must not say such things to me. In the first place, it is not true. I am not above the ordinary and also I must tell you that I am more or less betrothed to Sir Henry Riddick.'

105

'What do you mean by "more or less"?' he asked quietly.

'It was arranged by my parents when I was born and it seems to be accepted that I will marry him one day.' Cecily's tone had become flat; there was a sound of dismay in her voice and she sat on the sofa and looked down at the floor.

Max stood looking down at her and found himself thinking of her as a damsel in distress. Should he come to her rescue? No, he told himself, you cannot. You might have money, but you have no position in this country, no home or property, nothing to offer to any young lady.

He was saved from having to make a reply by the arrival of Freddy – a beaming Freddy who looked from his friend to his sister and smiled.

'You have met, but I must make the proper introductions. Cecily, my dear sister, meet Maximilian, Comte de Rochefort. Max, this is my sister, Miss Cecily Courtney-Welles.'

Cecily gazed up at Max. 'Are you really a count?' she asked breathlessly.

Max had to laugh and then to put the matter right. 'My father was Comte de Rochefort but he was killed in the Revolution. I have vowed to become a British citizen and the name I have chosen is Rockford. So I regret to say, my dear Cecily, that I am plain Mr Max Rockford.'

Freddy butted in. 'Just had an idea, Max: if you are going to change your name, why not become a Lidiard? That was your mother's name, after all.' He sounded enthusiastic but Max remained thoughtful.

'I think the first thing I must do is to find out if my grandmother is still alive. If she is, I must go and see her,' he said.

Freddy gave a broad smile. 'Just about to tell you. Discovered when I was in Dorset that she is alive and living as the Dowager Countess Hampton at Lidiard Grange. It is just on the border between Somerset and Devon, a village called Nether Compton ... and, Max, I saw your twin. I thought it was you, did I not Cecily? Nearly went up and spoke to you I was so sure, but could not imagine what you were doing there when I'd left you in London. Then I saw the difference: fellow had blue eyes, not your deep brown. Could have been your twin.'

'Cecily was just telling me. I wonder if it was one of my cousins. I should have several male cousins in Dorset. It would be interesting to find out.'

'Your grandmother would tell you.'

Max nodded. 'Yes, I think that must be my first task now that my leg has mended. Thank you for finding her whereabouts for me. Do you think I should get the stage there?'

Freddy was emphatic. 'Not a bit of it. You can have our second carriage. Father always did insist on a carriage for me but I prefer a phaeton in London. You might just as well travel in comfort. It's a good road as far as Shaftesbury, but it gets narrower after that.'

There was much argument but the matter was settled between them. By the next morning, Max found himself loath to part from Cecily and he held on to her hand for a long time before making his farewells and going round to the stables.

'Cecily, it has been very nice to meet you. I hope to see you again on my return from the country. I know I should not say it but don't forget me.'

Cecily, well on the way to losing her heart to him, reached up and kissed his cheek. 'There, that was a sisterly kiss, it is all I am allowed.'

'I will take a proper kiss when I return,' he said with a grin. 'Don't run off and marry Sir Henry Riddick while I am away.'

'Never,' she said stoutly. 'Not ever.'

Max enjoyed his journey across England. He was travelling in comfort and watched with interest as the landscape changed

before his eyes. Through Surrey and Hampshire, he was charmed
by small villages, then they made a stop at Salisbury and he found
time to visit the cathedral. He thought it was more beautiful than
anything Paris had to offer except possibly La Sainte Chapelle.

As they went farther west, the trees seemed to become more
golden and he knew this was the English autumn. Through
Shaftesbury, then as Freddy had warned him, the narrower and
more rutted lanes of Dorset and Somerset.

At Nether Compton, Lidiard Grange was soon found and Max
stopped with delight at the gates of a drive leading to the large and
rambling house; it was built in the local Ham stone and looked
mellow and welcoming. He hoped he would not give his grandmother too much of a shock.

He was shown in and was not quite sure how the maid had
announced him for in the drawing-room, he found an elderly
white-haired lady sitting at a writing-desk. She was very upright
and paused to look up with the pen still in her hand.

She gave a small frown. 'Good heavens, Max, whatever are you
doing here? Your cousin George told me you had fallen from your
horse and managed to knock yourself out. That does not sound
like you. He said you were staying with the Woottons at Wootton
Magna Hall so he was off to Weymouth for a spell. He spoke as
though he never went there . . . well, what are you doing standing
there without a word and looking awkward? Dressed to the nines,
too, that is not like you either and I swear you have grown since I
last saw you. . . . Well, say something for yourself, you have never
been lost for words.'

She put her pen down and looked at him and he saw a flicker of
doubt in her eyes. He himself felt almost scared, first his twin in
Dorchester and now his grandmother mistaking him for someone
else but calling him Max.

His grandmother, for it was indeed the Dowager Countess

Hampton now over seventy years of age but very hale and hearty, rose slowly from her chair and walked towards him.

She stood in front of him and had to look up at him. Her voice sounded shaky. 'I never have to look up at Max and his eyes are blue, yours are brown. What is this? Some kind of hoax? Some outrageous masquerade? Explain yourself please. Who are you?'

'I am Maximilian de Rochefort; your daughter Sophia was my mother; you are my grandmother.'

It was too much for the old lady. She sat down heavily on the sofa and reached for the vinaigrette.

Max stared at her in utter confusion. He was Max de Rochefort. Yet, here in England, there was another Max posing as himself? What did it all mean? He could not begin to work it out and was still at a loss for words.

But his grandmother was not slow in finding the questions that had to be asked. 'Can you prove that you are Maximilian de Rochefort? If you are indeed he, who is it who has been brought up by my nephew George all these years and also calling himself Max de Rochefort?'

He sat by her side and took her thin, wrinkled hand in his. 'I swear to you that I am Max. All my papers are in London; I had no idea that I would be doubted when I came here.' He held out his hand. 'Here is Mama's ring, I always wear it on my little finger because it is small. Do you recognize it?'

The dowager looked as though she had seen a ghost and she spoke in a voice that trembled. 'Her ring. My husband gave it to her when she had her first season, she was eighteen. That was before she met the Comte de Rochefort. I do not begin to understand this. If it is true and you are Maximilian, then there is something havey-cavey going on. Where have you been all these years, and what happened to your sister? Did she go to the guillotine with your parents as my Max has told me? I believe they called her Maxine which I always thought was foolish.'

'Yes, she died in the Revolution, Grandmama, I am the only one left.'

'And why have you come now? You managed to escape the Terror?'

He told her then and she listened to every word carefully. At the end of it, she spoke quietly. 'I believe you. I have to believe you; your story does not sound false and you have the brown eyes of your father and your mother's ring. But it only makes the mystery deepen. If you are Maximilian, who is the Max whom George brought back from France? Who has lived at Triscombe House all these years, who had his lessons with his cousins and then, instead of going to university, became George's steward? He has been a good steward. Who is he? I just do not understand.'

'Grandmama, there is only one thing to do. This Wootton Magna, is it very far away? I will go and confront this bogus Max and then I will come straight back and tell you.'

'How are you travelling, my boy?' she asked him.

'I have my own carriage; it is waiting outside.'

'It is only a few miles down the road to Dorchester; I will give you directions for your coachman. You will come back tomorrow and bring me news, won't you?'

'Yes, I promise. I will go straight away,' he replied.

'But I should have offered you some refreshment . . .' she started to say.

'No, thank you. I would rather be on my way to try and solve this mystery.'

And this was the story that Max told his sister after their reunion on that fateful day at Wootton Magna Hall. It kept Maxine awake half the night, but at dawn she fell into an uneasy sleep and then did not wake at her usual time. She was down to breakfast later than was her habit. She found that Gareth and Jessica had already left the breakfast-table and that only Sir Rupert was seated there.

She saw no sign of her brother.

His story so fresh in her mind, she greeted Sir Rupert with some reserve.

'Good morning, Sir Rupert. I have to make my apologies to you,' she said as she took her seat opposite him.

His reply surprised her. 'You called me Rupert yesterday.'

She flushed. 'It was forward of me, especially when I have deceived you all this time. I let you believe I was Max de Rochefort.'

Sir Rupert got up, walked round the table and sat himself beside her. He could not say what he had to say to her across a breakfast-table.

'Maxine. I say your name deliberately. You must admit that it is an easy transition to make. I think it is I who has to apologize to you.'

'Whatever do you mean?' she asked with a genuine curiosity.

'We have deceived each other. I have known all along that you are a young lady.'

'You mean. . . ?' She said it again but could not finish, as she felt she was blushing.

'On the day you held us up and Jem shot at you, we carried you into the carriage and I had to make sure that you had received no serious injury from the blast of the blunderbuss . . . no, please do not look embarrassed. I am the only one to know your secret. I undid your coat and shirt and, of course, I could see immediately that you were no young man. When I saw that the lead balls were only lodged in the shoulder pad of your coat, I extracted them quickly and made you neat again. Does no one else know your true identity?'

She was thankful for his quiet manner and nodded. 'Yes, Cousin

George knows and so does Mrs Turnbull, his housekeeper. We were going to be let it known when...' Maxine faltered. How could she tell this nice man that she was about to be betrothed to her cousin?

'Do not be afraid to tell me, Maxine,' he said softly. There was an affection in his eyes that was for her alone and she felt desperately in need of that affection.

'When I had finished my studies with my Lidiard cousins, Cousin George told me he wished to marry me. He had planned it that way all along... I always had a fear of it for I cannot like him even though it was he who rescued me and gave me a home.'

'Go on,' he spoke grimly.

'I refused him. I was only seventeen and I told him I would rather be his steward than marry him. He just laughed and said that would suit him. He would wait five years for me. And now I am two-and-twenty and he is beginning to think of marriage. I know he is.' She turned and looked at him. 'Now the real Max is here and that is wonderful, but it means I must become Maxine immediately. I hardly know where to turn.'

He would like to have shown her comfort but he could not as long as she was dressed as a young man, so he spoke boldly. 'Maxine, you are to do as I say. First of all, I would like you to tell me your brother's story, you can tell Gareth and Jessica later. Then you must decide what you are going to do about your cousin, and lastly, I insist that we spend a few days in Bath and purchase some gowns and dresses for you. ...'

'But you cannot, Sir Rupert.'

'Rupert, if you please.'

'I cannot allow you to buy me gowns, Rupert, it would not be proper. In any case, I am sure my brother will want to *sport the blunt* as you say. He has no property in this country, but all the de Rochefort fortune is lodged in a London bank. He told me so.'

112

'Very well, I will do as you say. But will you agree to the trip to Bath? I will rent a house for us all. I know that Jessica will love to help you at the milliners and mantua-makers in Milsom Street. Please ask Max what he thinks . . . ah, here he is.' Sir Rupert got up and greeted a handsome and well-turned-out Max who had entered the room.

'Good morning, Rockford. I know some of the truth but we shall soon learn the whole. I will leave the two of you together and Maxine will tell you of my plans.'

Max kissed Maxine on the cheek and sat beside her. She poured him some coffee and then told him of the conversation with Sir Rupert.

'He thinks I should become a girl immediately, Max, and suggests that we all take a house in Bath in order to buy the latest fashions for me. Would you be agreeable?'

'Most certainly,' he replied. 'We can't have the two of us going around looking like twins! But first of all, Maxine, we must go and call on Grandmama. She will be in a fidget to know what has happened. I think it will come as a nice surprise to her to find that she has both a grandson and granddaughter Rochefort. Will you let me take you to Lidiard Grange this morning and we can have a nuncheon with her?'

'Yes, of course I will, but I hope she will not be cross with me for deceiving her all this time,' said Maxine in a worried reply.

'I think she will be overjoyed,' was Max's opinion.

Before they set off for Nether Compton, the three Woottons and the two de Rocheforts sat together in the drawing-room and the whole story of Max's adventures was told right up until the time of the exciting reunion the day before, which had been witnessed by them all.

When the brother and sister arrived at Lidiard Grange, they found that Max had been quite correct about how the dowager would receive their news. She was so overjoyed to see them, she wept tears which had not been part of her make-up for a long time.

Max went in first to see her while Maxine walked in the sheltered shrubbery. They had agreed that it would be better to tell their grandmother the tale first rather than face her with two almost identical de Rocheforts.

As Max brought Maxine into the room, the dowager looked a commanding figure standing in the window.

'Stand together,' she ordered them.

They did and apart from their height and the difference in eye colour, there was an uncanny likeness.

'Bless me, you *could* be twins. It is quite true.' She smiled at them happily. 'Now, come and give your wicked grandmother a kiss, Maxine. Yes, I can tell which is you for you have your dear mama's eyes.'

Maxine gave the elderly lady and hug and a kiss at the same time; she, too, was smiling happily. 'You are not exactly a wicked grandmother, are you? You have been very kind to me all these years. I am sorry I deceived you and Cousin Rose for so long. I expect Max has told you why.'

'Yes, it is that rascal of a nephew of mine. I do not know what will become of him. Don't you agree to marry him, my dear, we will do better for you than that. And now I will tell you why I am wicked and then we will forget about it. I did not approve of my lovely Sophia marrying a French count in her first season. I distanced myself from her and her family, then when I was ready to forgive her, it was too late. That is my punishment and I must live with it and enjoy having you as my grandchildren. Oh, I know I have got Thomas's children and my great-grandchildren, but you two are very special to me. I would like to think you will settle in Dorset and visit me often in my remaining years. And how long are you going to be young man, Maxine? You really cannot go about looking the double of your brother.'

They told her of the Bath plan and she was enthusiastic.

'Excellent. A good man, Sir Rupert, I know of him. He, too, has his sorrows losing his wife so young. Perhaps you would do for him, Maxine.'

They all laughed. 'What will you say next, Grandmama?' Maxine asked her. She found that she liked the idea that Sir Rupert was approved by her grandmother and was left wondering why it seemed so important to her.

The brother and sister had a lot to tell their grandmother and they returned to Wootton Magna to make their preparations for the Bath visit.

EIGHT

SIR RUPERT DECLARED that the trip to Bath was an urgent one and their preparations were made that same day. His steward was sent out to procure a house for them and a note was sent to Triscombe House to say Max and Maxine would return there in a few days' time. Maxine had insisted that it was only polite to let Cousin George know of their Bath direction even though she had no idea when he would be returning from Weymouth. She wrote to him briefly of her brother's arrival and of her intention of ending her masquerade and becoming a lady.

The following afternoon found the Woottons and the de Rochefort brother and sister settling into a solid and rather elegant house in Bath's South Parade. It was near the centre of the city and from its upstairs drawing-room windows, which were ornate with balconies and blinds, there was a good view of the more fashionable of Bath's visitors as they took their morning parade. It was considered a prestigious address as it was near the river, not far from Sydney Gardens and was favoured particularly because it was away from the noise of the carriages.

Maxine herself was feeling neither pleased nor excited. Sir Rupert had insisted that she should squeeze herself into one of Jessica's dresses with a pelisse over her shoulders. Although Jessica

117

was very much the same build as Maxine, she lacked her height and a dress which neatly reached Jessica's shoes was woefully short of Maxine's ankles.

Jessica, however, was triumphant and took Maxine into the drawing-room to show her to Sir Rupert.

'Papa, look, Maxine looks very well, does she not?'

But Maxine could not agree and stood awkwardly and miserably in front of the gentleman she admired so much.

'Sir Rupert, I cannot be seen like this, not even by the modiste. What shall I do?' She looked at him fearfully but he was smiling. Maxine's skin had never suffered exposure while she was wearing a gentleman's garments and to him, she looked soft and pink and very alluring.

'You look charming, my dear. Leave it to me. I will make up some story by the time we reach Madame Juliette. She will be a great help to you. She knows me well as I often visited her with Margaret.'

Maxine knew Margaret to have been Rupert's wife and put up no more protests. 'Very well, I will do as you say, but I feel very strange.'

'In a day or two, you will have forgotten that you were ever a young man. All the beaux of Bath will be admiring you.'

'You like to roast me,' she said, but she smiled at him.

Madame Juliette was pleased to greet such an old customer and such a valued one. She guessed that the tall and good-looking Maxine might be the next wife of Sir Rupert and that she must do her best.

She listened to his story sympathetically. Maxine also listened with some awe and amusement at Sir Rupert's imagination and invention.

'Dear madame,' said Sir Rupert pleasantly. 'May I present to you Mlle Maxine de Rochefort. She is lately arrived from France and has survived a calamity. She crossed the Channel in a sailing vessel which came to grief near Weymouth and she has lost all her possessions, even her travelling dress was ruined. She has borrowed a dress from my daughter, Jessica, whom you know well. But as you can see, it is a sad fit. I know you will come to our rescue. If you have one dress and perhaps a pelisse she could walk away in and if I may leave an order for a complete new wardrobe for her, I would be most grateful.'

Maxine looked at Sir Rupert in astonishment and then their eyes met. She saw the laughter, and had to return his mischievous expression and try to show her thanks.

'You are very kind, Sir Rupert.'

'Not in the least, it is a pleasure. I will leave you both here for the afternoon and come back for you before dinner.' He turned to Mme Juliette. 'Do you think it can be done, madame?' he asked.

She was wreathed in smiles. 'For you, it shall be done, Sir Rupert. I have a dress almost finished which will suit admirably, and I will call in an extra seamstress to make the complete wardrobe for *mademoiselle*. We will take the measurements this afternoon and Mlle de Rochefort can choose some silks and muslins. By Saturday, she will be fit to take Bath by storm!'

There followed what Maxine afterwards thought of as an outrageous afternoon and she was glad of Jessica's help – and her admiration. She was quite bewildered by the finest silks from the East and the dainty cotton muslins which she thought she could never wear. Not an item of apparel was left out, and from the linen-draper next door, she obtained gloves and stockings, reticules and muffs.

When Sir Rupert returned, Maxine approached him with delight. She was wearing a dress which was of the blue of her eyes and she held herself proudly. I am a lady now, she thought, it feels rather strange and slightly wicked.

119

Rupert Wootton was shaken as he took her hand in his; he had known Max to be a handsome young man, but he had never expected such proud beauty in Maxine. He had thought she would be awkwardly aware of her change of sex. He had reckoned without Madame Juliette's artistry and Maxine's determination not to shame him.

'Maxine.' He took her hand. 'I had not expected such beauty.'

She laughed merrily. 'Not beauty, Sir Rupert, but Jessica says I look well and I certainly feel very different.'

'You will have all of Bath at your feet,' he said.

'Roasting again,' she quipped and from that moment, she began to enjoy herself.

At the house in South Parade, Max was expecting her and he, too, was all praise for her looks, but Maxine thought she could detect a note of sadness in his voice.

'You are lovely, Maxine, just like Mama. She was never to know how we would be when we were grown up.' Then as a thought struck him, his tone lightened. 'Grandmama is going to be very pleased with you.'

'Yes,' agreed Maxine. 'I am glad of that.'

For the next few days, they spent their mornings having a look at Bath which they thought was a very gracious and agreeable city. Maxine had only the one dress, but by the time Mme Juliette had worked her magic, Sir Rupert declared that they should go to the Assembly Rooms. Cousin Elsie would be with them so it was all quite proper for him to escort his guest. In any case, he told Maxine, she had the company of her brother.

When Maxine appeared in the drawing-room at South Parade on the evening of her first ball, she found Sir Rupert on his own and was at once smitten with unexpected shyness. He was dressed magnificently and looked young.

Maxine had chosen an even paler blue for her ball gown and the low bodice had little embroidered knots of silver. Her only ornament was her mother's cross around her neck and no argument from Jessica and Cousin Elsie would make her change it for a necklace. Her dark hair was still cut boyishly short, but Jessica's lady's maid had succeeded in coaxing it into a few ringlets.

'Maxine.' Rupert glanced up as she entered the room and knew he had met his fate. But he must tread very carefully.

'Sir Rupert.' She made a little curtsy as Jessica had taught her.

'No, no, it must be Rupert.' He was holding both her hands and she could see the admiration in his eyes. Admiration and something else, but she could not begin to wonder what that might be.

'Thank you for bringing me to Bath, Rupert. I know that you have agreed with Max that all the bills should be sent to him, but it was you who had the idea of coming here and taking this fine house.'

Rupert was stirred both by her beauty and his own feelings, but he tried to keep the conversation in a mood of light-hearted badinage. He failed miserably.

'Do I get a thank-you kiss?' he asked her and he could have bitten out his tongue for his foolishness. He could see the colour rising in her cheeks. She is not ready for flirting, he thought.

But Maxine was looking at the face of her kind protector and reached her lips to his. It was meant to be the lightest of touches, an expression of gratitude, but once their lips met, neither of them could draw apart. And neither wanted to.

It was the sound of Jessica's merry voice at the door which parted them, but not before Rupert had lifted Maxine's hand and kissed it lightly. She was glad he had done it because it seemed to tell her to ignore the message of their embrace, to tell her that they would return to their happy friendship of the past few days.

At the Assembly Rooms that evening, Maxine felt a tremor of nervousness. It was not that she was unused to such scenes for her cousin George had often accompanied her to similar occasions at Weymouth. But then she had played the male and and had been used to accompany young ladies in the country dance or the quadrille. She had never danced the waltz.

Her nervous tremor lasted for about two minutes, for she was introduced to so many exquisite gentlemen and friends of the Wootton family, that she was immediately requested for every dance.

That was except for the waltz and here an argument ensued between herself and Rupert.

'I knew you would be a success,' he told her, as she was escorted back from a country dance to her place at the side of the glittering ballroom. 'And now, I insist that you dance the waltz with me.'

'No, Rupert,' she said very seriously. 'I do not dance the waltz.'

He looked at her. Beautiful and with a set look of determined obstinacy in her face, he guessed that those qualities had seen her through many awkward moments when she had been posing as a young man.

'Do you mean you cannot dance the waltz, or you will not?' he asked quietly, yet keeping his voice light.

'I cannot.' She looked up at him. She was seated and he was standing in front of her. He had to fight back an impulse to put his lips to the very spot on her shoulder which he had first seen in strange circumstances in the dim light of his carriage only a few weeks before. 'You must realize that when I attended balls before, I was the male partner and I refused to dance the waltz with a young lady. It seemed a terrible pretence and so I have never learned it.'

'You can learn it now, in that case,' he said, and, as she looked up at him, she could see that he really did mean his words.

'How?' she asked, even though she knew what the answer would be.

'I will teach you. I am considered to be a fine dancer of the waltz.' There was a smile about his lips and in his eyes as he looked at her. 'Come along, it is about to be announced. I like the idea of having my arm about your waist.'

'Rupert!' she protested.

'Maxine,' he answered with some aplomb. 'I will go very carefully around the edge of the ballroom and you will soon learn the steps. I will not allow you to refuse, you know.'

His hand was on hers and she was being pulled to her feet as he heard the master of ceremonies call the waltz.

The floor was not crowded as some mamas still frowned upon the waltz, so there were many envious glances from young ladies who longed to be whisked round the floor in the arms of a young gentleman.

Maxine loved the rhythm of the music for it seemed to dictate the steps to her and Rupert guided her expertly over the floor.

'Look at me,' he said suddenly.

And she looked up and found him smiling at her. At the same time, her feet seemed to know what to do and she knew she had learned to waltz. It was a thrilling moment and she breathlessly enjoyed the rest of the dance.

Rupert did not take his arm from her waist as he led her back to her seat and she was suddenly aware of the tightening of his fingers and a slowness in his step.

'What is it?' she asked immediately.

'Your cousin George has arrived. He is talking to Max and the look on his face is thunderous.'

'Oh, what shall I tell him?'

'Tell him you are betrothed to me,' he said quickly, and almost under his breath.

'But I am not,' came back her reply.

'You could be.'

'Balderdash, do not talk such nonsense. Leave me to handle my cousin.'

'Very well, I accept your refusal of my kind offer but I will stay near you.'

'Rupert, there are times when I cannot take you seriously, but here we are . . . Cousin George, what brings you to Bath?'

'You do. What is all this I hear?' George Lidiard was dressed in a coat of a garish puce which would have seemed stylish on one of the dandy set twenty years younger than him. He was glaring at her and she could see both anger and resentment in his eyes.

I must stay cool, Maxine said to herself. 'You have met Sir Rupert Wootton, I believe. He was very kind to take me in when Remus threw me. And I did send you a message to tell you that my brother Max is still alive: is it not wonderful after all these years?' She turned to Max who was watching her with amusement and admiration. He had received a grilling from George while Maxine was enjoying the waltz and had taken an instant dislike to his cousin. 'Max, you have introduced yourself to our cousin? He has given me a home all these years, but of course, this is the first time he has seen me dressed as a lady.'

She looked at her cousin who seemed as though he was about to have apoplexy. 'Well, Cousin George, I did write and tell you I was to become the lady. Do you admire me?'

She saw George try to take a hold on his temper. 'It is obvious that I must now call you Maxine, my dear cousin,' he said stiffly. 'I am pleased to make the acquaintance of your brother and to know he is safe. You need no longer make your pretence which has been very useful to us.' He turned to Sir Rupert. 'I am staying at the White Hart Hotel; if you will permit, I will call on my cousin in the morning. Now, Maxine, how about standing up for the country dance with me. It is nearly the end of the evening.'

Maxine glanced at Rupert and he gave a slight nod.

So she looked at her cousin and spoke politely. 'Yes, of course, George, we have a lot to talk about. You will know how excited I am to find my brother still alive after all these years.'

The evening ended without further incident, but next morning, Maxine found herself not looking forward to Cousin George's arrival. She had an instinctive feeling that the meeting was going to be an awkward one.

Max and Gareth had gone riding and when Jessica heard George Lidiard announced, she left the drawing-room to Maxine. 'You will wish to see your cousin on your own, Maxine, you can tell me about it later. I will go and seek out Polly and ask her to accompany me to the Circulating Library; Papa says that I must not venture into the city without a maid.'

'He is quite right, Jessica,' replied Maxine hastily. She did wish to see her cousin on her own.

George's coat was of a sober hue compared to the puce affair of the night before, but Maxine thought he made a ridiculous figure.

Maxine was in a sprig muslin that morning and the weather being much cooler, she wore a shawl of fine Cashmere around her elbows. Her hair had been dressed becomingly and her carriage was such that her tall, slender figure was not dwarfed by the burly George Lidiard.

He blustered from the start as though he had been done a grievous injury. 'Well, my goodness, Maxine, I never thought to see you in such looks. I hope you will not be seen flaunting your new found beauty at the Pump Room.'

'Jessica and I have been in the habit of taking a walk there, Cousin; Max and Gareth usually accompany us.'

'Max. Dammit, I am yet to hear the whole story. You had better tell me of his miraculous resurrection.'

Maxine tried to keep a hold on her temper. 'It is like a miracle, is it not? A brother I thought I had lost all those years ago, suddenly to be amongst us again. It is still all quite amazing to me.'

'And it seems his coming has forced your tranformation into a beautiful young woman. I could not believe me eyes – or my luck – when I entered the Assembly Rooms and saw you dancing the waltz with Sir Rupert Wootton.'

She looked at him closely and did not like the expression she could detect in his eyes. He was behaving politely enough but she knew that she could see both greed and lust in his eyes. It was going to be difficult to keep him at a distance. But she had to question one part of his remark.

'Why do you say "my luck", Cousin George?'

He drew nearer and she could almost feel his eyes creeping under the low neck of the muslin. She shifted her shawl a little higher and it was the wrong thing to do.

He put out a hand and whisked it from her arms letting it fall to the floor. 'No, do not hide your charms, my dear, I wish to see what will soon be mine. And Max tells me your father made a settlement for you; it is not the fortune I had hoped for but it will keep me comfortably. But I will be the possessor of your tempting beauty, that is my luck.'

Maxine froze. She had half-expected such words but they had been said in such an intimate way, that she feared the worst. 'What is your meaning, Cousin?' she said frigidly.

He laughed and putting out his fingers, he stroked her cheek then let his hand rest on her bare shoulder. 'Why, Maxine, my sweet child, surely you realize that this means that you must become my wife without delay.'

Maxine stared. She knew his meaning well enough, but he spoke as though she had no option but to become his wife immediately. And the last thing in Maxine's mind or in her plans was to become the wife of her detestable cousin.

'I have no intention of ever becoming your wife, Cousin George.'

She did not know if his look of surprise was feigned or deliberate, but he gave a short laugh. 'But of course you will be my wife. I have always planned it so, and now you have no option.'

'Why have I no option? You have been good to me but I am not bound to you,' she said, keeping her voice steady.

George leered at her. There was no other word, she decided, and she awaited the worst. 'You are bound to me, Maxine my sweet cousin, you are bound to me by the laws of convention. By the laws of decorum, call it what you will. You have lived in my home as a female all these years with no chaperon. Now that it is known that you are a lady, you have no choice but to marry me. If you refuse, your reputation is in ruins. You have been compromised. No gentleman would look at a girl who had spent five of her adult years under my roof. They know me, you see.'

Maxine turned aside. Tears pricked her eyes; she felt a heavy sickness rise in her. All the happiness of Max's appearance and her transformation into a lady vanished. Can he be right? Do I really have no option? Fearful thoughts came to her and the tears disappeared and her temper rose.

She turned to him swiftly. 'I will never marry you. I would rather stay a compromised spinster all my days than be married to you. If it shows ingratitude then I am sorry. You have used me to suit your own ends but I will not bow to your demands, Cousin.'

'Hoity-toity,' he sneered. 'Have you not reckoned that even the so-called kindly Wootton family will have no more to do with you when I spread it around that all the time you were my steward, you were also my mistress?'

Maxine never knew how it happened, but she raised her arm high and dealt her cousin a hard, stinging blow across the face.

He reeled and went scarlet at the same time. 'How dare you,

127

harlot,' he screamed at her and, seizing her in his arms forced a passionate kiss on her. She struggled and her dress in disarray, she sprang apart from him.

'I'll have the better of you, Cousin George,' Maxine shouted at him, suddenly knowing that she might be able to gain the upper hand over him.

'Gammon,' he shouted back. 'You are disgraced and will be mine. There is nothing more to say. I will obtain a licence and we will be married in Bath Abbey tomorrow.'

Maxine steadied her nerves and her cunning. 'Do you mean you would not mind being married to a woman who is a common highwayman, *a gentleman of the road*?'

He seized her arm but she did not flinch and stood her ground. 'What are you saying?' he gasped.

'Have you had time since your return from Weymouth to notice that The Elms and Downs Farm both have new thatch?' she shot at him.

'I did see it and I am not in the least pleased that you have spent my good money in my absence; you know that I had refused you to get the thatcher in.'

'I have not spent any of your good money, as you put it. I would not have dared. I had other ways of securing the money.'

His eyes fixed on her. 'What do you mean? You have never played the harlot and been paid for your services?'

Maxine laughed then. The idea was ludicrous but typical of her cousin. 'You have no need to insult me, George. No, your masquerading cousin turned highwayman and robbed the rich to pay the poor, as they say. Did you not hear of several hold-ups on the Dorchester road? Why we had one ourselves, did we not? It gave me the idea.'

His fingers were tight on her arm and she winced with the pain of his grasp. But she did not look away; she had the feeling that she had succeeded in her ploy.

'You are lying to me,' he hissed at her.

'I tell no lies, Cousin George, I have the new thatch to prove it. I obtained enough money in two hold-ups to give each farm a new roof. Unfortunately, I was greedy. I came to grief on my third venture.'

'What are you saying now?'

'I had the misfortune – or the stupidity, call it what you will – to hold up a carriage with a groom sitting beside the coachman holding a blunderbuss. He shot at and missed me as it happens, but the shock made me fall from Remus and I was knocked out. Fortunate, was it not, that the owner of the carriage was Sir Rupert Wootton himself, and he kindly took me into his home until I recovered. He knows the whole story.'

She looked at him and could see he had no words to say to her so she pressed her advantage. 'As you now know, I was at Wootton Magna when my brother – the real Max – appeared and I was forced into becoming the lady. Quite charming, am I not?'

Maxine thought that her cousin would have seizure or an attack to the heart. His face was purple with rage and he was speechless. Then the words burst out, just one at a time.

'Reprobate – hussy – hoyden, there is no word to describe you,' he stuttered.

'So you have no wish to marry such a person, Cousin George?' Maxine deliberately turned sweet, she knew it would enrage him further.

'I will marry you, damn you. I will not be put off by your wicked ways. Perhaps it will add spice to our marriage. And I will make sure you will never marry the like of Sir Rupert Wootton, if that is what you are planning. Your name will be disgraced throughout the county and you will only have me to turn to.' He stopped, then as an afterthought, he shouted as he left the room,

'And what I am to do about a steward, damn you?'

Maxine managed a grin in spite of the turmoil of her feelings. 'You will have to spend a little less on gambling and your dear Diana,' she mocked. 'Then you will be able to employ a proper steward, Cousin George.'

'Be damned to it, I will have you as my wife and you can still play the steward until we set up our nursery.'

And he stormed out, leaving Maxine weakly laughing yet trying not to burst into tears.

NINE

ᘻAXINE HEARD HIS quick and furious step on the stairs and the slam of the front door below. Her tears flowed then. They were partly of relief that he was no longer in the house.

Jessica heard him leaving, too, and, peeping into the drawing-room, saw the weeping Maxine and being a sensible girl, ran to find her father.

Sir Rupert came immediately and seeing the woebegone Maxine sitting on the sofa staring vacantly in front of her, he crept into the room. But the click of the door behind him was heard by Maxine and she turned her head sharply in the fear that it might be her cousin returned.

But when she saw that it was Sir Rupert standing there with a look of grave concern on his face, she got up without thinking and threw herself into his arms.

He held her tightly to him and then guided her back to the sofa. 'Hush, my little love,' he whispered, but she was so distracted she did not hear the words. Afterwards, he thought it was just as well.

'Has your cousin gone, Maxine?' he said aloud, possessing himself of both her hands in his.

She clung to him and her composure partly returned. 'Rupert, there is nothing for it. I am disgraced. I shall have to marry my cousin. There is no way out of the coil I have got myself into.'

'Tell me,' was all he said.

Their eyes met and she knew she could not tell of her dilemma to a better person.

'I have told you that Cousin George had always planned to marry me and that I managed to defer the evil day by becoming his steward. Now it is all undone. He says my name is disgraced because I have lived with him all these years at Triscombe House without a chaperon. And now that it is known that I am a lady, I am compromised. Then I was foolish, Rupert, I thought it would give him a dislike of me so I told him how I had become a highwayman. But it did not work.'

'What did he say?' Rupert asked quietly.

'He said . . . oh, I cannot say it . . . he said it would add spice to being wed to me. He said he would spread the word of my actions throughout the county and that no one would look at me. I would *have* to turn to him.'

An arm came round her shoulders and Maxine found herself with her head against Rupert's waistcoat. He was stroking her hair gently.

'It would make no difference to me. I would look at you, Maxine.' The announcement was clear in the silence of the room and she sat up alarmed.

'Fustian,' she said with some of her old spirit. 'I am no longer fit to stay under your roof.'

'That is for me to say,' he said firmly. 'Become my wife, Maxine, that would silence George Lidiard for ever.'

She moved apart from him so that she could see his face. She thought he looked grim. She did not know that the grimness was there because of his murderous feelings for George Lidiard. What was in his heart he had not mentioned.

'Oh, Rupert, you are being kind to me. You know very well that I could never marry you. George is right, as much as I hate to say it. I have been living in his house as a young woman without a chaperon of any kind. I have been naïve, have I not? I imagined that because I was dressed as a young man and was his steward, I was safe. I never once thought of the impropriety of it. After all, he is one of my nearest relations, or I thought he was until Max came. And now he knows how I got the money for the thatch. I never meant to tell him. But I was so angry that I thought it would give him a distaste of me. It was just the opposite. How can I have been so stupid?'

'You have not answered my question,' he said firmly.

'What was it?'

He had to smile within himself; never had a proposal of marriage gone so completely disregarded, he thought. I must try again.

'Will you marry me, Maxine? I am asking you to be my wife.'

Maxine was silent for a long moment. He is asking me to save me from George, he does not love me. I cannot go from one loveless situation to another. I am much too fond of Rupert for that.

'I will have to say thank you, but decline your kind offer, Sir Rupert,' she replied formally.

'Am I too old for you?' he asked.

She looked at him astonished; his distinguished features, his intelligent eyes, his firm but kind mouth. He might be the father of Gareth and Jessica but to Maxine, he seemed to be the ideal age for a husband. So she smiled at him at last.

'Too old? I know you are older than me but you are yet young. George is much more than twice my age . . . he is horrible. Oh, Rupert, you are so kind to want to save me from George, but I cannot let you bear my disgrace. I cannot bring shame to you and your nice children.'

133

While she was speaking, he had drawn her towards him so that his face was close to hers. She met a look in his eyes which seemed to tell her many things; she longed to return his feelings but knew she must deny him.

'Rupert . . .' she whispered, ready to tell him she could never marry him. But the words were not allowed to come.

His lips were on hers and were telling Maxine in no uncertain terms that he loved her. She felt the warmth, the passion. She could not stop herself from returning his kiss, she did not want to stop herself, she wanted to stay there for ever. . . . Then as the sweet kiss ended, the memory came to her of another kiss so brutally taken. And George Lidiard was there between her and Rupert Wootton. She might come to love Rupert in time, but he could never be for her.

And she jumped up and made for the door. 'I can't,' she was muttering feverishly. 'I can't, Rupert. I must marry George. I am sorry.' And she ran from the room.

In the drawing-room, Sir Rupert had not moved. He banged his clenched fist into his hand. Fool, he called himself. You have been too hasty. I know now that I love her and want her for my wife, but how can I keep George Lidiard's hands from her? I have rushed her and lost her for the moment, but I will work on a way of getting her cousin out of the picture. I must go very slowly and tactfully but I will win her in the end.

Both Maxine and Rupert made their plans for the future.

Maxine, in the quiet of her bedroom, threw off her gloom and guilt over the behaviour of her cousin. Perhaps I may never have to see him again, she told herself, and the thought pleased her. I will ask Max to take me to Grandmama; I am sure she would give me a home. And Mrs Turnbull can send over my few possessions and I will have no need to see Cousin George again. The thought cheered her, though she was sorry to desert the Grattans and the

Lockyers at Triscombe House. I did my best for them, she tried to assure herself.

For his part, Sir Rupert decided that the time had come to remove to London for a while and he determined to make Maxine one of their party. It will serve to help her forget her dreadful cousin, it will be company for Jessica, and it will give me the chance to make myself better known to her.

It was all accomplished within the sennight. The visit to Lidiard Grange was made and Sir Rupert was introduced to the dowager who was pleased to make his acquaintance and delighted at Maxine's plan to go and live there. But she insisted on her having a London season first. Jessica was excited at the thought of them being in London even though her come-out season would not be until the following year. Gareth and Max, by now as thick as thieves, planned visits to White's and Tattersall's and succeeded in enlisting Freddy Courtney-Welles to make up a trio. Max also hoped to further his cause with Cecily, but kept these plans to himself.

The Woottons' town house was in a neighbouring square to that of the Courtney-Welles' which delighted the young people. The smaller house which belonged to the dowager was not far distant, but Maxine made the decision to stay with the Woottons. Moving into Lidiard House would mean not only having to find a chaperon, but to run the danger of meeting Cousin George; he was accustomed to using the London house from time to time.

As long as she was with the Woottons, she would have the chaperonage of kind little Cousin Elsie who doted on Maxine after the excitement of her becoming such a lovely young lady. To Cousin Elsie, it was all very romantic and she nourished a secret hope that perhaps Maxine would become the next Lady Wootton.

Maxine, Cecily and Jessica soon became known as the Inseparables. They did everything together and made a becoming trio. Usually they had Freddy, Max and Gareth in willing attendance, but as these young gentleman often preferred a visit to Jackson's Boxing Saloon to a promenade in St James's Park, their ways often diverged. On these occasions, the willing Cousin Elsie would accompany the young ladies.

The one thing they did all join in together was the morning ride in Hyde Park; Sir Rupert had his own London stables and provided mounts for the two de Rocheforts.

It took only a few days for Maxine to realize that Freddy Courtney-Welles seemed to be forming an attachment to her. She had taken an immediate liking to the young man who had been her brother's companion in the Peninsula; he was of a sensible nature but also possessed of a rather wicked sense of humour and fun. His company and his conversation helped to make Maxine throw off her worries over her cousin George.

Maxine never did find out how it happened, but the story of her playing the highwayman became one of the *on dits* of the town. And Freddy was intrigued by such a beautiful young lady carrying out such a daring venture.

He arrived at the Woottons' house in Suffolk Square one morning accompanied by Cecily who was immediately snapped up by Jessica; Max would have preferred a private conversation with the young girl he knew he was coming to love.

They were all in the drawing-room, but Freddy secured Maxine for himself on the small ottoman. She was looking very pretty, her hair was longer and hung in natural curls which softened the strong features of her face.

'Maxine, what is this story that is going about town?'

Maxine looked at him and saw a curious and rather wicked look in his eyes. 'Freddy, whatever are you talking about? Has Prinny been up to some other indiscretion, or is it still Lady Hertford?'

'No, no, not the Regent, I think he is at last going to separate from Mrs Fitzherbert. It is *you. . . .*'

She looked at him in astonishment. 'Fiddlesticks, how can there be any talk about me? I am not known in town.'

'I think your cousin George must have spread the tale. It is going around that you played the highwayman and held up a carriage in Dorset.'

Maxine flushed scarlet. Surely her misbehaviour in the country had not followed her to London?

But Freddy could see the embarrassment on her face. 'It is true, I can tell by your expression. Maxine, what a jest. Do tell me the whole. I could fall in love with a lady who dared hold up a carriage at pistol-point. Did you have a pistol?'

'Freddy, Freddy,' pleaded Maxine. 'I cannot deny it, but I will only say so to you because you are my dear friend and because you took care of Max after Talavera. But, Freddy, you must know that I did not do it as a prank.'

He lifted her hand to his lips. 'Tell me.'

So Maxine told him the whole and he gave a sigh. 'What a marvellous girl you are, Maxine. I have never met anyone like you. Wouldn't think of marrying me, would you? Never thought to be leg-shackled, but to have a wife who once posed as a highwayman . . . it beats everything. . . .' Freddy found himself speechless.

And Maxine laughed and laughed. 'Oh, Freddy, you really are a case and I love you for it. You have no intention of being wed but you would marry me because I held up a carriage at pistol-point! I could kiss you, Freddy,' she added.

'I don't mind, would be a privilege.'

She laughed afresh and leaned across and touched his lips with hers. 'There you are, now you can say you have been kissed by a highwaywoman if there is such a person – perhaps a lady high-wayman would sound better. And it shows just how improper I can be to kiss you when we are in the drawing-room and in company!' She stopped her laughter and looked at him again. 'But, Freddy, how has this tale got about? Max or Rupert would never have mentioned it. Do you happen to know if my cousin is in town?'

'George Lidiard, you mean? Believe I met him at White's. Bit of a freak, ain't he? Dresses as though he is the latest dandy and looks about the same age as Prinny.'

Max sighed. 'That is George. I hoped to have escaped him for a little while. I shall kill him if he is circulating this tale.'

Freddy pretended alarm. 'No, don't do that, Maxine. Don't mind a highwayman for a wife, but not a murderer.'

And they laughed together until Max broke off his conversation with Jessica and Cecily to come and ask what all the fun was about.

Maxine was to meet her cousin that evening. They had all been invited to a private ball and halfway through the evening, she caught sight of George across the room. His dress was in a quieter mode than usual though his neck-cloth was extravagant and his shirt points high; she thought he looked quite handsome. He came over to her. It was the first time they had met since their quarrel, but George seemed to have forgotten his threats and was at his most affable. She somehow distrusted him. Thankfully, he did not seem quite so loathsome.

'My dear Maxine, how lovely you look. I congratulate you on your success. I hear that the highwayman story has got about. . . .'

'You did it, Cousin George. It must have been you who has spread the tale.'

'Not guilty, dear Coz, more likely to have been Sir Rupert, I should think. You must realize that it does not reflect well on me.'

She did not believe him and said so. 'I do not trust you, George.'

'Never mind, come and stand up for the quadrille and we will forget our differences and again become the friends we have been all these years. Proud to have such a beautiful woman as my cousin.'

'I am not taken in by flattery, George, you must know me better than that.'

Maxine felt a little relieved that her quarrel with her cousin seemed to be over and was civil to him during the dance. For the time being, at least, he seemed to have put thoughts of marriage from his mind.

A few minutes later, she found Sir Rupert by her side. 'Come to supper with me, my dear,' he said. 'I must hear if you have managed to forgive your cousin. You seemed on good terms with him.'

She put her hand on his arm and walked with him, to the refreshment room. 'Rupert, I must tell you, the highwayman story is going the rounds. George said he did not start it, he thought you must have done so. Is it true?'

Rupert Wootton looked at the girl who had become so dear to him; he had laid his plans and had given the young people free rein. He had been pleased to see Maxine so taken with Freddy Courtney-Welles, whom he knew would be a harmless rival and a good friend to her. The laughter he had observed between the pair was just what Maxine needed. But now George Lidiard was on the scene again and Rupert could see trouble brewing.

He laid his hand on her arm and through the fine lace of her long glove, he could feel the warmth of her. 'Maxine, will you trust me? I want you to believe me. I have said nothing of your past. I would protect you as I would my own children. You will come to no harm from any carelessness from my tongue. Look at me.'

She looked up and once again met eyes which held a message she was not ready for. 'Rupert, you are my good friend, I do know that. Yes, I do trust you. It is my cousin I cannot trust. He is suddenly very polite which is suspicious in itself. Am I wrong to feel like that, Rupert?' she applied to him.

'I do not think so. Be on your guard with him and come to me if you need help. Enjoy yourself with Freddy and the other young people. What do you think of Max and Cecily Courtney-Welles? Look at them now, they are sitting at that small table in the corner.'

Maxine was glad to have the subject changed and looked across the refreshment room. True enough, Max was sitting with Cecily and they were obviously very happy in each other's company.

'It would be nice, would it not?' said Sir Rupert.

Maxine gave a little frown. 'Yes, I would be happy for them though you *do* know that Cecily is spoken for? And I do not want Max to mislead Cecily. I know he is calling himself Mr Rockford, but he is still a de Rochefort. However, he has no standing or property in this country, you know. I think he feels the lack of it.'

If Rupert and Maxine had been able to eavesdrop, they would have been able to hear Max and Cecily having a very similar conversation.

Max had resumed his friendship with Cecily after his journey into Dorset and did not find himself changed in his opinion of her. That she adored him could be seen at a glance.

'Cecily, I have not known you for many weeks and we have had this separation. I have come back to London to find you as lovely as ever and I want to tell you that I love you.'

Cecily was torn in two. Pledged to Sir Henry Riddick, but in love with this young man so recently arrived from France. What was she to do? She was a simple girl and her reply was straightforward and honest. 'I am not free to tell you that I love you, Max. My feelings are not engaged to another, but officially I am to marry Sir Henry Riddick. I do not think you have met him.'

Max stiffened. He knew of Sir Henry and the little he did know was enough to tell him that the baronet would not do for Cecily. He also knew that he had been wrong to tell her that he loved her. Although possessed of a private fortune, he had no position or home in the country to offer her.

He spoke slowly. 'I know Sir Henry only by repute and believe him to be a respectable gentleman but no longer young; he is in possession of a large estate in Hampshire and in need of an heir.'

Cecily flushed, but she appreciated his plain speaking. 'I know he is no longer young; he is the same age as Papa which is about forty-eight, in fact. I do believe he is the same age as your cousin, George Lidiard and that they are close acquaintances. I do not love Sir Henry, but I have a respect for him and it would be hard to go against my parents' wishes.'

She felt his hand placed on top of hers on the table. 'I cannot bear to think of you married to him, Cecily, but I have nothing to offer you. I am little more than a soldier from the Peninsular War. I would like to offer you marriage, but you are committed and I have nothing to commend me.'

'No, no, Max, do not speak like that. I will not let you. You are a de Rochefort whatever you chose to call yourself in the Peninsula. And you are still *Le Comte*, even if your home is in England now. I am proud of you, Max.'

His hand tightened over hers. 'Are you saying that you love me, Cecily?'

She smiled gently and nodded. 'I loved you as soon as I met you, Max. I shall always love you even if I have to marry Sir Henry.'

Max stood up. 'We will find a way. Do not ask me how. I will speak to Maxine and you will speak to Freddy and between us we will find a solution.' He put his hand gently on her shoulder. 'We cannot declare our love, my little one, but we can hope. Come back to the ballroom and we will dance the waltz together to show that we are not downcast.'

And so it was that the three young gentleman put their heads together over the problem of Cecily's commitment to Sir Henry Riddick. They came up with a preposterous plan.

It was now into November and they had only a few weeks before they would all be going to their respective country homes for the Christmas festivities.

It was Freddy who put the plan to Cecily. Jessica was there, too. Maxine was driving out with Sir Rupert, and Freddy was glad of this as he thought she might have frowned upon the idea even though it was for the sake of her brother's happiness.

Freddy and Cecily were paying a morning visit to the Wootton house and found Jessica on her own. Gareth and Max had repaired to Jackson's for a sparring match.

'I am glad you are here, Jessica,' said Cecily as they entered the drawing-room. 'I was feeling mopy this morning and you always cheer me.'

Freddy thought this was a good start and ploughed straight into his mission. 'Are you still in a fidget about your attachment to Sir Henry, Cecily?'

Cecily looked at her brother; she loved him dearly and could always confide in him. 'I cannot like the match, Freddy. You have known that for ever. But neither can I go against Papa's wishes. Sir Henry is his closest friend and he has waited all this time for me. Now that I am eighteen, I believe they are going to hasten the marriage and I find myself at quite a turn.'

'You don't love Sir Henry?' Freddy knew what her answer would be but he was wanting to draw Cecily out. He was sure she loved Max, but she was not a disobedient girl and would want to conform with her parents' wishes.

Cecily looked both penitent and scornful. 'Of course I do not love him. I have a regard for him and he is all kindness, but he is so elderly, Freddy.'

Freddy laughed. 'I don't think he would like to be called elderly; he would think he was in his prime at forty-eight. I think he would be more comfortable with that relative of his who keeps house for him. A distant cousin, I believe, but she is his age and I should think he has had her devotion for ever.'

But Cecily could not laugh. 'He promised Papa, you see,' she said gloomily. 'What am I to do, Freddy?'

Here is my opening, thought Freddy, I will take the plunge. 'Do you love Max, Cecily? Does he love you? I believe it to be so.'

Cecily flushed scarlet and looked confused. Although she was his little sister, Freddy thought she looked adorable and he could understand his friend falling in love with her.

'Well, Cecily?' he asked lightly.

'Oh, Freddy, I do love Max and he says he loves me. But it is hopeless. I am tied to Sir Henry so what can I do? Max says he has no status in this country and cannot offer for me. I think that is balderdash. I would still love him if he was the youngest son with no competence at all.'

'Cecily,' said her brother firmly, 'if we managed to get Sir Henry to back down, it would be easy to get Max to offer for you. We have only to persuade him to become *Le Comte* again – he is very wealthy, you know. I think our parents would be impressed. They do want to see you comfortable.'

Cecily laughed for the first time. 'It is kind of you to think of it, Freddy, but I cannot see any way of making Sir Henry change his mind. Unless you could think of one of your wicked plans like you used to do when we were children and we got into scrapes.'

'I *have* thought of a plan,' said Freddy stoutly. 'Or I should say that Max and Gareth and I have thought of a plan.'

143

'Oh, what nonsense you do talk. But I can imagine the three of you hatching some kind of plot. I will allow you to tell me.'

'I will tell both of you for this includes Jessica as well, so I am glad she is here.' He looked at Jessica as though seeing her for the first time. She was only seventeen but destined to become a beauty, he thought. 'Are you willing to give your support to Cecily, Jessica?' he asked her.

Jessica was near to adoring the fun-loving Freddy and would have done anything he asked her. 'Oh yes, Freddy, you can rely on me. Absolutely,' she added.

He nodded his approval. 'Good girl; now, listen carefully, the two of you. Sir Henry is a very proper gentleman. We have known him all our lives and have always liked him; he has almost been as an uncle to us, I should say . . . you are smiling, Cecily, what have I said?'

'I can hardly marry an uncle, Freddy,' she grinned, already feeling cheered and hopeful.

'Exactly. As well as being proper, he is very serious. He studies history and archaeology as a pastime and although he is Father's friend, he does not frequent the coffee houses—'

'Freddy, hurry up. Whatever has all this to do with his commitment to me?' Cecily interrupted.

'Be quiet and listen,' said her brother. 'As I see it, and Max does, too, the last thing Sir Henry would want in a wife is a giggly, silly schoolroom miss—'

'But I am not a schoolroom miss, and I am not silly or "giggly",' protested Cecily.

'Be quiet, you will not let me tell you the whole,' thundered Freddy and Cecily knew she must take heed. He was doing this for her. 'The idea is for you and Jessica to play the simpering misses when Sir Henry is there. Be as childish as you like, say silly things, talk about the latest fashions or something like that, anything that would make him think that you were the last thing he would want in a wife.'

Cecily looked at him in awe. So did Jessica.

'Freddy, did you and Max plan all this?' asked Cecily.

'My idea,' claimed Freddy. 'Max willing to agree, thinks it might do the trick. What do you say to the plan? Could you do it?'

Cecily looked at Jessica and her friend gave a cheeky little smile and nodded.

Cecily got up and kissed Freddy. 'I could hug you, Freddy. It might work and it would not be doing anything dishonest. But, Freddy, we have got to get Sir Henry to come to the point first.' Cecily was suddenly serious.

'Thought of that,' replied Freddy promptly. 'You go and tell Mama that you and Max love one another, that you do not wish to marry Sir Henry.'

'And how will that help?'

'Mama will have the vapours, then she will tell Papa and they will have Sir Henry round to make his offer for you in no time at all. When he comes, all you have to do is to play the pretty widgeon, a pea-goose, whatever you like as long as you are not serious. Give him a dislike of you instantly.'

Cecily did look serious for a moment, then her face brightened. 'I could try it and Jessica will help me, I can tell by her expression. You think it a good jest, don't you, Jessica?'

'It would be easy,' replied Jessica without hesitation. 'We can giggle over a fashion book at any time, indeed we often do when we see some of the preposterous styles in *The Ladies Monthly Museum* or *La Belle Assemblée*.'

They made their plans and the very next day, Cecily approached her mama. Mrs Courtney-Welles was a sympathetic and loving mother; having lost six of their offspring in babyhood, she was deeply attached to both Cecily and Freddy. She had been happy with the arrangement made with Sir Henry Riddick though there were times when she would wonder if the studious Sir Henry was quite the right choice for the young and lively Cecily. But it was her husband's wish and as her children knew, she would never go against her husband's wishes.

Cecily hoped to see her mother on her own before her friends arrived to take her riding and, as it transpired, she was provided with an opportunity the very next morning. The breakfast-room hardly seemed a suitable place, thought Cecily, as she came down-stairs, but it so happened that day that her father had gone out of the house early on a business matter. Freddy was nowhere to be seen and Mrs Courtney-Welles and Cecily were able to take their tea and toast together in quiet comfort.

'Mama, I am glad that Papa has gone out as there is something private I wish to speak to you about,' said Cecily with a quiet determination.

'What is it, my love?'

'It is the matter of my attachment to Sir Henry Riddick.'

Her mother nodded. 'Yes indeed, Cecily, you are now of an age for us to be able to make the arrangements for your marriage. Your papa and I have been talking about it.'

'I do not wish to marry Sir Henry, Mama.'

The words were out and Cecily watched the bewildered look on her mother's face.

'But, Cecily, you have always known that you were to be the wife of Sir Henry. What has happened to make you think other-wise?' Her mother's voice was faint.

'I have fallen in love with Max de Rochefort.'

Her mother looked horrified. 'But he is nobody in this country, a dispossessed count from France. It is your duty to marry Sir Henry, Cecily, your father would say so, I know. I do believe he will say that the time has come for Sir Henry to make you a formal offer. Then we can begin to arrange the marriage, perhaps for next spring.'

'I do not wish for it, Mama,' persisted Cecily thinking that the conversation was going exactly as she anticipated.

'I hope you will obey your papa, Cecily. I will speak to him on the matter.'

'Yes, Mama,' said Cecily meekly and thought that Freddy would be pleased with her.

TEN

$\mathcal{T}$HEY RODE IN the park later that morning and as Cecily wished to tell Max of the morning's developments, Freddy rode with Jessica leaving Maxine to challenge Gareth to a race. The two of them had been fond of a gallop together at Wootton Magna and although it was frowned on in the park, they both liked to disregard the polite rules.

Before the morning was over, Freddy made sure of a word with his sister. 'You have spoken to Mama?' he asked Cecily.

She nodded and gave a chuckle. 'Yes, I lost no time and I have a feeling that Sir Henry will be making a morning call tomorrow. I must make sure that Gareth brings Jessica in good time and does not go off to his favourite sport.'

'I will go and fetch Jessica,' said Freddy promptly.

Cecily grinned. 'She likes you, Freddy.'

'I know she does, it is quite diverting. I am not usually considered one for the petticoats,' he replied.

'I expect you make her laugh; she is very young.'

Freddy considered. 'She is eight years younger than me but at least she is out of the schoolroom. I am sure she has enough wit to help you out with Sir Henry, Cecy.'

'We will see how it turns out tomorrow.' she said with a good deal of confidence.

As it happened, the next morning all the friends were gathered at Courtney House. Max had arrived with Maxine who for once was not riding with Sir Rupert, and when Freddy went to fetch Jessica, Gareth insisted on going back with them to see the fun, as he put it.

Fortunately, the drawing-room was large and when Mr Courtney-Welles brought Sir Henry Riddick into the room, they were met by a happy scene. Neither had any idea that it was deliberately staged.

Maxine was seated at the pianoforte – she had taught herself while she was acting the young man at Triscombe House and was accomplished; Gareth stood at her side and turned the pages of the music of a Mozart sonata. Jessica and Cecily, both very pretty and girlish in their sprig muslins, were on the sofa with a fashion book on their knees, while Freddy and Max were engrossed in a game of backgammon.

Mr Courtney-Welles felt proud that he was bringing his friend to such an engaging gathering.

There was no denying that Sir Henry Riddick was a distinguished-looking gentleman and a member of one of the country's leading families. Approaching fifty though he was, his tall build offset his tendency to portliness. He was dressed to a fault in white pantaloons and a dark-blue coat made by Weston, his waistcoat being of a lighter shade of blue and very plain. His eyes proclaimed the intelligence of the scholar and many people would have regarded him as an excellent prospect for a young daughter.

'Cecily, my dear,' said her father. 'Sir Henry has come on a morning visit. He has known you all your life, but I expect you are aware of his kind intention towards you.'

The young people held their breath wondering if Cecily could rise to the occasion.

Cecily dutifully got up from the sofa and made her curtsy to Sir Henry's rather stiff bow; she let him touch her fingers.

'Oh la, Sir Henry,' she trilled – there was no other word for it – 'You have come just in time for me to show you the latest fashion from Paris. Jessica and I have been giggling over some of the modes for they are outrageous.' She turned and picked up the fashion book to show him. 'Do look at this gown, is it not splendid? And so low in the bodice, I do think it would be declared indecent at Almack's. And as for having plumes of gold all around the hem, I never saw the like. Do sit down so that we can look at it together – it is sure to amuse you.'

Freddy afterwards was heard to say that the expression on Sir Henry's face had to be seen to be believed.

But Jessica, as prearranged, moved from the sofa and let the would-be suitor take her place.

'Very interesting, Miss Cecily,' he said. 'I had not thought you to be a young lady influenced by the current fashions.'

'Oh, Sir Henry, you cannot know me. Whatever is the latest, even if it is quite ridiculous, I must have it. Last week, it was little pearls sewn in hearts all over the skirt – it was delicious, I think that is the only way to describe it. And my mantua-maker sewed one of my dresses in the style in a single morning.' She stopped to look up at him; his face was a study of bewilderment and kind understanding. 'I do not know but I am sure that the craze will have quite disappeared by this week and it will be something equally foolish.'

There was an awed hush in the room at this inspired performance by Cecily. Only her parents were frowning; Freddy said later that they looked as though they had bred a monster.

Into the silence came Sir Henry's polite and dignified voice. 'And do you read, Miss Cecily? Do you like books?'

Cecily's smile was radiant. 'Oh, I do indeed, Sir Henry. My friend Jessica – she was sitting with me but she made room for you – Jessica and I read every single story from *The Ladies Monthly Museum*. And I have read every tale of Mrs Radcliffe. Do you know her, Sir Henry? You must have read *The Mysteries of Udolpho*. I know it is her most popular novel, but it is *The Romance of the Forest* which is my favourite. And then there is Mrs Edgeworth, she is very proper and I have *Belinda* which I consider to be the most romantic. . . .'

Cecily turned to Jessica. 'Do you remember *Belinda*, Jessica, and how we loved that scene in the garden?'

Jessica smiled but her reply was serious. 'I think that Sir Henry would consider that the books of Mrs Hannah More were reading better suited for you, Cecily.'

'Yes, you are right, Jessica,' Cecily replied, and looked at Sir Henry again. 'But, sir, I would not like you to think that I spend all my time reading. I ride in the park every morning, then there are the loo parties, but I do not gamble heavily, you can be sure – I am most careful when it comes to money. I believe I spend more on new bonnets than on anything else. Of course, the evenings are taken up with routs and parties, so many invitations, and I have to turn down a lot of them. Do you dance the waltz, Sir Henry?'

It was enough, and they all watched as Mr Courtney-Welles, his expression almost black with rage, escorted his guest from the room.

As the door shut behind them, there was a roar of laughter. Freddy picked up Cecily and whirled her around. Max came over and kissed her on the cheek. And Gareth stood in the middle of the room saying 'Do you dance the waltz, Sir Henry?'

They all declared that Cecily had surpassed herself and it was only Max who seemed not quite so euphoric.

If they could have heard the conversation between Sir Henry

and Cecily's father, they would have been more than pleased.

In the library, the two friends sat facing each other across the fireplace. 'Arthur,' said Sir Henry to Cecily's father, 'we have always agreed that I would make an offer for dear Cecily when she was eighteen, but I am afraid it will not do. She is a very pretty, bright little girl, but alas, she is not in my style at all. As you know, I am very studious and not given to novels and dancing. I fear we would not suit. Find one of those nice young men who were there with us in the drawing-room, a friend of Freddy's perhaps. Was there not a young Frenchman he met while he was in the Peninsula? His father a count or something. That would suit Miss Cecily much better and I will settle for my faithful Freda who has kept house for me all these years. She is neither young, nor a beauty but she understands me. Please give my regards to Mrs Courtney-Welles, I am sure she will appreciate my feelings.'

As soon as Sir Henry had left, Cecily was summoned to the library. She knew her father would look serious but he was not as angry as she had feared she might be.

'My dear Cecily, I think your success with your friends must have gone to your head. I had thought my daughter to be more serious but it seems I was wrong. Freddy was always the clown of the family and I love him dearly, but I had always thought my dear little Cecily to be just the one to suit my old friend Henry but I was mistaken. Come and give me a kiss and we will forget all about it. Henry says he will marry his cousin which I think will suit him better for she is used to his ways. And I suppose I shall be having a visit from this young Frenchman, though I do not know if it will do. He is not established in this country, you know. Run along now and tell your mama what I have said.'

Cecily felt like giving him a childish hug but she merely thanked him, kissed his cheek and ran from the room. She knew she must find Max.

But Max de Rochefort – or Rockford as he still insisted upon – had a dilemma. He had watched Cecily demolish the suit of Sir Henry and had been amused and delighted. He guessed that the older gentleman and long-time friend of the Courtney-Welles family would withdraw his claim immediately.

This could only mean that Cecily, his dearest love, was free to marry him. But how could he apply to her father with nothing but his fortune to commend him? He knew Mr Courtney-Welles to be of the strictest principles and could guess that it would need more than money for him to give permission for his daughter to wed.

Cecily had run from the library and Max had left the drawing-room. There was a half-landing and a tall window on the stairs, and here they met. Cecily's eyes were shining with excitement.

'Max, oh Max, I was coming in search of you. Such news. Sir Henry has withdrawn his suit and is to marry his cousin. I am free, Max. Do you not think that I played the part of a little flibbertigibbet very well?'

He took her hands and smiled at her. 'You are nothing but a minx. I could hardly believe it was you. You really did not mean all that stuff about the latest fashions, did you, Cecily?'

She shook her head with a laugh. 'I can assure that I do like to dress well and I am outrageously expensive for only the best will do! But I am really very conservative in my choice of a dress or gown. As long as my dresses are nicely made and I am not the dowd, then I am satisfied. Does that please you?'

'It is not up to me. You must aim higher, Cecily; you deserve someone with more standing than I have.'

She stared at him. 'What are you saying? I am free now and I am acting shamelessly. I am almost telling you that you might offer for my hand.'

He pulled her up against him and bent and kissed her quickly and softly on the lips. 'I love you, Cecily, and I would like to be able to make that offer, but for the moment, I cannot.'

'You are turning me down,' she said stonily.

He managed a laugh. 'No, it is not like that, Cecily. You must be patient and see if I can find a means of making my way in this country. I read for the law in Paris, maybe I could become an English lawyer or a Member of Parliament. If I can do that then I will go to your father. Would you accept me if I was a lawyer?'

She laughed merrily. 'I would accept you if you were the gardener, Max.'

'I do not think it will come to that. Tell me, do you go into Somerset for Christmas?'

'Yes, we do. Would you come with us? I could ask Mama.'

He shook his head. 'No, I am sorry, I am committed to being in Dorset with Maxine. We go to visit our grandmother.'

'I believe her to be a formidable lady; she will help you, Max.'

'She is getting old, it is up to us to help her, Cecily.'

'So it will be several weeks before I see you again,' she said to him, but she did not sound dismayed for hope was strong in her young heart.

'Once the better weather has come, we will be back in London again. We have that to look forward to.'

'Yes, we have, Max, you are quite right; and I shall have Freddy. He is always cheerful. Max, you don't think Freddy would do for Maxine, do you? Then it would be a match between two brothers and sisters.'

He shook his head. 'No, I think I know where her heart lies but she is bound to our cousin George. He seems to be set on marry-ing her.'

'Oh dear,' she said in a quiet voice, then brightened. 'Perhaps we could think of another prank like this morning's.'

'No, we cannot, you moppet. Once in a lifetime of a scene like that is enough. I will have to keep you in order.'

'I have not given you the right, you will not let me.'

'One day perhaps, Cecily, one day.'

Maxine had been an onlooker in all this, but she could not disapprove of the capers of the young people. She knew only too well what it was like to have the threat of having to face an unsuitable marriage hanging over one's head.

Rupert had asked her to drive with him in his curricle out to Richmond Park and she was pleased to accept. She longed to tell him of the charade in the drawing-room when Sir Henry Riddick had come courting Cecily.

The traffic was light and having a crack hand with the whip, he was able to listen to her story as they drove along. Across the park, he drove more slowly as he watched her face.

'Are you happy about Max and Cecily?' he asked her.

'Yes, I am, but I do not see how it can be resolved. I am sure they love each other and I would be pleased to have Cecily as a sister. She is a dear girl. But Max is by no means sure of himself. He still calls himself Rockford which I can see was necessary in the army, but I do think he should return to our family name. There is nothing to stop him being the Comte de Rochefort, but I know of his feelings on the matter. De Rochefort is a French title and England is at war with France. I think Max is being too sensitive. There are many French families settled in this country since the Revolution and they are accepted amongst the *ton*. You only have to think of the Duc de St Julien and his family. And in any case, Rupert, we must never forget that our dear mother was English.'

Rupert was thoughtful. 'Perhaps your grandmama will have something to say on the subject. Do you see her soon? I have been wanting to ask you. Are you to spend the Christmas season at Lidiard Grange with the dowager or would you like to come to us at Wootton Magna?' He paused. 'It would give me the greatest of pleasure, Maxine.'

She turned her head to smile at him and caught the expression she was coming to know so well. It could not, it must not be for her. But she was able to answer truthfully. 'Grandmama is expecting the two of us. So Max must be parted from his Cecily, and I will be parted from you, Rupert. I am sorry.'

He took hold of her hand and let the reins lie loosely in the other. 'Are you really sorry, Maxine? Or are you being polite?'

She would not let her heart speak for her; she would not even listen to its urgings to become closer to Sir Rupert Wootton. 'I *am* sorry, Rupert, I love it at Wootton Magna.'

But he was not satisfied with her reply and leaned across and sought her lips. He let his passion flare quickly and ruthlessly and Maxine knew she was giving him the answer he was seeking. But she would not say it in words. Still she denied him. 'I think it *is* a good thing I am going to be with Grandmama for the festive season, Rupert. I must not let you think that I can ever be more than a dear friend.'

And Rupert had to be content. Her lips had given him his answer. He did not want her as a dear friend but as a passionate and loving wife. There were many obstacles but he would take his time and overcome them until she was his.

The friends split up and went their separate ways with their families.

Before Max and Maxine left the Woottons, she received a visit from George who was preparing to go to Triscombe House.

'Maxine, are you sure you will not come to Halstock? It will be quite proper if you have Max with you and you will be able to see your cousins at Lidiard Manor.'

Maxine looked at him. He is being very formal for George, she told herself. Perhaps he has forgotten about me being his wife; I have seen little of him of late. He is probably going to his lady-love in Weymouth.

So she spoke politely. 'Thank you for asking us, Cousin, it is kind of you. But Grandmama and Cousin Rose are expecting us. Perhaps we will see you there? It is not very far from Halstock.'

'Maybe, Maxine, maybe, but I will not promise. I will look forward to seeing you again in London when the season resumes after Christmas.'

By this time, Max had bought his own carriage and a fine pair of greys which were kept at stables not far from Suffolk Square. Sir Rupert had spared one his stable boys to act as coachman and the journey into Dorset was made in comfort and with no severe weather to hamper them.

At Lidiard Grange, they were gladly welcomed by their grand-mama and even Cousin Rose seemed animated with pleasure. Although there was no riding done by either the dowager or Cousin Rose, they found that two fine hunters had been procured for their use during the holiday.

It was a few weeks without routs or parties or balls, but Maxine found that she liked being in the countryside and espe-cially enjoyed her morning ride with Max. They did little visiting except when they all got into the carriage to be taken to Lidiard Manor.

Maxine had long talks with her grandmother and was pleased to find that the highwayman story had not reached the dowager's ears.

It was inevitable that the conversation should turn on to both George and Max, and Maxine told her grandmother of her brother's predicament.

'Grandmama, Max is putting on a cheerful face for your sake, but I must tell you that he is quite downcast and at a pass. I wish you would talk to him.'

So the tale of Max's love for Cecily was told and the dowager greatly enjoyed the pantomime of the severance of Sir Henry Riddick's offer for Cecily.

'Do you think Cecily the right one for Max then, Maxine?'

'Yes, I do. They are a very respected family, the Courtney-Welles.' You may not know them as their country home is in Somerset, near Taunton, I believe,' said Maxine.

'I recollect that I knew Mrs Courtney-Welles' family before she was married,' replied the dowager. 'High sticklers they were, too, but pleased with the match. Now what is this all about? Max is good enough for the Courtney-Welles' any of these days. Tell me the problem.'

It took a long time to tell her grandmother of Max's worries, but Maxine was careful to give her own opinions, and then waited for the reply.

There was a long silence.

'Maxine, you have given me a lot to think about. I have some ideas on the subject, but I need to consider them carefully. Leave it to me and I will have a talk with Max.'

Maxine gave her a kiss and smiled gratefully. 'Thank you, Grandmama, I knew you would help us.'

The next evening, when Max had joined them after dinner, the dowager sent Cousin Rose and Maxine off to the library to hunt for a novel of Tobias Smollett which she seemed to have mislaid. Maxine went willingly on this pretext, meaning to tell Rose all about it and not to go back to the drawing-room until they were called. There was a fire in the library so they were quite snug and Cousin Rose was a willing recipient of Maxine's explanation.

Max himself watched his sister and his cousin leave the room and gave a little frown.

'Did you wish to see me on my own, Grandmama?' he asked

her. He respected both her views and her outspokenness and wondered if he was in for a grilling.

'Tell me about the Courtney-Welles', Max,' the dowager began autocratically.

Max was startled. This he had not been expecting.

'I met Freddy at Talavera, Grandmama; we were in the same brigade and both of us injured. My leg was broken and no one could have been kinder than Freddy. He kept up my spirits all the time we were waiting to be taken to the hospital at Lisbon. He was injured too, but not so badly and we stuck together after that. It seemed natural when we arrived in London that I should go to his house. That's when it all happened!'

'What happened, Max?' she said, knowing very well what his answer would be.

'I met his sister, Cecily. I fell in love with her straight away. I knew then there would never be any one else for me.'

'And she fell in love with you?' she asked quietly.

'Yes, but it was hopeless.'

And the dowager was told the story of Sir Henry Riddick all over again. She smiled and nodded.

'So your Cecily is free now. Have you made her an offer?'

'I cannot. I am quite wealthy, Grandmama, but I feel that her family would not agree to her marrying a French *émigré* with no estate and no prospects. . . .' He stopped appalled by what he had said. 'Oh, Grandmama, I am sorry. That must sound like a criticism of you.'

'But you are right, my boy. I would not accept your mother's choice of husband and I have paid dearly for my prejudice. I never saw my dear daughter again and almost lost my grandchildren. Max, listen to me if you can bear to take heed of foolish old lady. You are now the Comte de Rochefort; not Robespierre, not

Napoleon, and no Englishman can take that away from you. And never, never forget that your dear mother was English. She was the Comtesse de Rochefort and you are her son. No one is going to forget that you are partly a Lidiard and you must be proud of that.' She paused and tried to read his expression. He looked very serious and earnest.

'Give up this Rockford nonsense, that served you while you were fighting the French but it is at an end. I want you to stand up as the de Rochefort I never allowed my daughter to be. Do it for my sake if not for yourself and your Cecily.'

Max got up and paced about the room. The dowager countess thought she had overdone it.

Then he turned to her smiling. 'I have been a fool, Grandmama. I could only look back and see the disasters of the past. I cannot forget the guillotine, you know, and how Mama gave me the chance to escape. I owe it to her to do well. The Lidiard family are all hereabouts. I can set myself up as a lawyer in Sherborne or Yeovil and buy a house nearby so that we will be close to you.'

She, too, was smiling and it was with relief that she had succeeded in turning his mind. 'You have no need to buy a house, Max.'

He came and stood looking down at her. 'What are you saying?'

'This house has been in the Lidiard family for generations and I would like it to be yours. If you marry your Cecily, I will have it made over to you as my wedding gift. No, don't say anything until you have heard the whole, for there are some conditions attached. This is a large house with many rooms unused. It will come to you as long as you can agree to have me and your Cousin Rose living here for as many years as are left to me. After that, Rose will go to her sister and it will become your family home. Don't look so astonished. It would give me the greatest happiness to know that

161

it was going to my Sophia's family. Well, what do you have to say, young man?'

He stooped and kissed the lined cheek. 'You have left me without words, Grandmama. You are all kindness. How can I refuse such an offer? I hope we can both make up for each other's sadnesses. I will put it to Cecily. I think she will be delighted for she told me that she would marry me if I was a gardener! I think a country lawyer living at Lidiard Grange will be an improvement on that, don't you? And I think, Grandmama, I will call myself Max Rochefort and forego the title. I have to consider myself as being English from now on. You will not disagree?'

'No, of course not, if it is your choice. There, we have it all settled. But there is still something I wish to ask you.'

'What is that?' He sat by her side again.

'It is Maxine. I can say this to you. I do not wish her to marry her cousin George. He has a bad name in the county and he keeps a mistress in Weymouth ... no, you needn't look scandalized, I may be an old lady but I am aware of these things. I know he is my nephew but he is no suitable husband for Maxine. What can we do? What can *you* do? What about Sir Rupert Wootton, is there any chance there, do you think?'

Max spoke slowly. 'It is my opinion that Maxine loves Sir Rupert even if she is afraid to admit it to herself. Cousin George has a dreadful hold on her, you know. And it is quite true that she lived with him all those years without a chaperon.'

'Can you bring to bear on her? Can you and your friend Freddy think of some ruse to bring Maxine and Sir Rupert together? You were successful with Sir Henry Riddick!'

He laughed aloud. 'Grandmama, you are wicked and you have a naughty sparkle in your eye. I will put it to Freddy and we will see what we can come up with. Freddy is very fond of Maxine.'

'I will leave it in your capable hands. You are to write and tell

162

me what you are up to. It will be an amusement and a relief to me.'
She leaned over and reached for the bell-pull. 'I will ask for the
tea-tray to be brought in and you can go and fetch Maxine and
Rose.'

ELEVEN

THE FAMILIES IN Dorset and Somerset lingered in their country houses until the middle of February. There had been heavy snow in January and travelling was made difficult.

As the thaw came and the days got longer and lighter, the Courtney-Welles', the Woottons and Max and Maxine found themselves as part of the London scene once again. George Lidiard, of whom they had seen little, had also removed to town.

Max and Maxine still declined to stay at Lidiard House with Cousin George and were made very welcome in Suffolk Square.

Max's most urgent and immediate task was to present himself at Courtney House and seek an interview with Mr Courtney-Welles. He did not see Cecily first for he wanted to be proper and knew that he should ask her father's permission before he addressed himself to her.

Unknown to Max, Mr Courtney-Welles had been making enquiries into the young man's background. It only needed the knowledge that Max was the grandson of the fifth Earl of Hampton and that his mother was one of the Dorset Lidiards for him to decide that the young man seemed to be a suitable husband for his daughter. He had resigned himself to the fact that Sir Henry

Riddick would not have done for Cecily; he put his daughter's happiness before anything.

Max was shown into the library and invited to sit by the rather meagre fire – this fact being more because it was early morning than for any mean-fistedness on the part of Mr Courtney-Welles.

He greeted Max heartily. 'Well, young man, I am going to call you Max because Cecily must have mentioned your name at least a hundred times a day while we were down in Somerset. I am sorry you could not be with us, but I can understand you wanting to visit your grandmother. My parents were acquainted with the fifth earl.'

Max was amused at this for it seemed to signify that family connections were worth more than any fortune. He began to wonder if he was to be given a chance of saying anything, but he was relieved at what seemed a warm and friendly reception.

'Thank you, sir, we have enjoyed several weeks with my grand-mother and she asks to be remembered to you. It seems that Grandmama knew Mrs Courtney-Welles' family when Cecily's mother was still a young girl. She knows of my intention of seek-ing you out to ask for Cecily's hand in marriage as soon as I arrived back in the capital. My grandmother is very pleased at my choice and has been most helpful and generous. I must tell you that I am possessed of a comfortable fortune from my father's estate; also that I am resolved to become a lawyer in Yeovil or Sherborne. You will wonder why I have chosen these West Country towns, but the truth is that my grandmother is handing over her home at Lidiard Grange to me as a wedding gift. It is a substantial house and lies only a few miles from each of these towns. The house itself lies just on the county border and I think it would make a delightful home for Cecily and myself if I succeed in my suit. We would also have the use of the Lidiard town house here in the city.' He paused and saw that Mr Courtney-Welles was listening seriously.

'I have gone on at length because I wished you to know the full extent of the provision I can make for Cecily. I love her dearly and hope you will give your permission to ask her to do the honour of becoming my wife. I should also tell you that I will become Maximilian Rochefort. I wish to keep the family name, but will not style myself *comte* in this country.'

Max drew breath. He could not remember speaking to anyone so formally and at such length and looked at his prospective father-in-law anxiously. To his relief, he saw that Mr Courtney-Welles was smiling.

'Excellent, my boy, you have done well to secure Lidiard Grange which will make a fine home for you both. It is not so far distant from our country home, I am pleased to say. We are honoured to have a de Rochefort for a son-in-law and I know that this is going to make Cecily very happy.' He stood up and offered Max his hand. 'Off you go now, and find the little girl. Maybe Mrs Courtney-Welles will be able to prepare a celebration of your betrothal in a few days.'

They shook hands and Max left the library; he could not reach Cecily fast enough. He guessed that she would be anxiously waiting in the drawing-room, having been told of his interview with her father.

He stopped abruptly as he stood in the doorway of the room for Cecily was there, but with her mother.

Mrs Courtney-Welles must have seen the expression on Max's face, for she stooped and kissed Cecily on the cheek. Then she hurried forward and took Max by the hand. 'I can see that my congratulations are due, but they can wait. I will leave the two of you together. I do not think that you have any need or any wish to have a chaperon.'

As the door was shut, Cecily hurled herself into Max's arms. Neither of them spoke for Max claimed his first real kiss of passion and they stayed locked in each other's arms for many minutes.

Then she took his hand to lead him to sit very close to her on the ottoman. 'Tell me,' she whispered, and her face was flushed with excitement.

'Oh Cecily. I do love you so much and want you for my wife more than anything else in the world. Your father was most agreeable. Will you say yes?'

She put her lips to his and they were almost caught up in another web of passion, but she broke away so that she could speak to him. 'It is my wish too, Max. I do love you. Do I have to be a gardener's wife?'

It was laughter and delight from then on as Max told her of the plans which had been made.

'How does all that suit you. Cecily? Will you mind living at Lidiard Grange with Grandmama and Cousin Rose for a few years? I can assure you that the house is so big that we will be able to have one wing of it for ourselves.'

'Your grandmother has been very kind and I know I shall love her. Is there a big estate, Max?'

He shook his head. 'No, the house is set in formal gardens but nothing more. If you do not object, I will pursue my career in the law.' He stopped and gave a laugh. 'Do you know, Cecily, I will have to go back to being a student for a little while before we marry. It is French law I am trained for and I think things will be different over here. I had not thought of that before. I will study in London for a few months and we will plan a summer wedding. Would you agree to that, my sweet?'

She gave a long sigh. 'I am so happy, I would agree to you learning to be a chimney-sweep, I do declare. Max, shall we go and find Freddy? He is going to be so pleased.'

Three days later, they all met at Courtney House for an informal party to celebrate the bethrothal. The gracious house boasted a small ballroom and there they gathered. Mr Courtney-Welles gave a long speech extolling the virtues of his daughter and Max gave a short speech of thanks which was constantly heckled by a Freddy who had, drunk too much. No one heeded him and it was a happy occasion.

George Lidiard had been invited and attached himself to Maxine. He, too, had drunk liberally and was most convivial.

'Maxine, it seems that marriage is in the air. I have not seen you since before Christmas, how was Grandmama? She has done very well for Max. I must say I had hoped of Lidiard Grange coming to me one day. But I surrender it gracefully. I have Triscombe House and Halstock is nearer to Weymouth which suits me very well. How about the two of us being wed at the same time as Max and Cecily? It would make a double wedding for the Rochefort brother and sister which would be rather nice. What do you think?'

Maxine looked at him suspiciously. She knew he had been drinking, but for once it had not made his behaviour objectionable. His tone was quite mellow. She wondered if he would stay mellow when she gave him her reply.

'Cousin George, you know very well that I have no intention of marrying you. You threatened to tell tales about me, but I can assure you that they will not hurt me. I have every intention of remaining a spinster and I shall take great delight in being an aunt to the growing family of Max and Cecily.'

He gave a short laugh. 'You are too beautiful to remain a maiden lady, Maxine. If I put my mind to it, I am sure I will be able to persuade you to be my wife. But there is no hurry, though your portion of the Rochefort fortune is tempting. I have you within my grasp for you could not survive the tale I could spread about you.'

169

'You are as wicked as ever underneath your charm, Cousin George, is it any wonder I do not wish to marry you?'

'You will marry me in time, I am quite certain. You will be glad to.' And he gave a short laugh which spoke of self-satisfaction and success. 'I must see if I can have a word with Max, I have yet to congratulate him. He has done very well for himself. Are you going to give me a kiss?'

'George, we are in company; what will you say next?'

He grinned at her. 'Do you mean that if we were not in company, you would let me kiss you?'

'No, I would not. You do not have to be told that.'

'Ah, Maxine is being very proper. I will take my kiss nevertheless.' And he bent his head towards her and his lips touched her neck fleetingly just at the point where it sloped to her inviting shoulder. 'No, don't fly into a huff. I can see Sir Rupert making his way towards you. He guards you very zealously, damn him.'

Sir Rupert was indeed at her side and he looked as though he expected to find her angry.

'What did your bounder of a cousin want? He was very familiar, was he not?'

Maxine laughed. 'Oh, Rupert, that is his style. Nothing will change George. He was quite amiable, though he still threatens me with a scandal. He asked me to marry him.'

'Did he indeed? And what was your reply?'

'I always refuse and tell him I would rather remain a spinster than be married to him. He did not seem in the least put out. I am sure he has got something up his sleeve; his face looked as though he was hatching some ploy to make me say yes.'

Rupert put a hand on her arm. 'Come into the drawing-room with me, we will be quieter. All this celebration is very noisy!'

Maxine laughed but she followed him for she wanted to be on her own with Rupert. She had not yet asked him what he thought of Max and Cecily's betrothal.

The drawing-room seemed strangely quiet but it was well lit and warm and they sat themselves near the fire.

'Are you pleased about Max and Cecily?' he asked her.

She smiled. 'That is what I wanted to ask you! They seem very happy, do they not?'

'Max could not have made a better choice and I was pleased to hear of the settlement with your grandmother, Maxine. It will be good for her in her remaining years to have them with her.'

'Yes, I am pleased. It will make up for her heartbreak over Mama, even though I know she brought it on herself. It has all worked out very nicely.' Maxine smiled at him.

'I wish it could work out just as nicely for Max's sister.'

'What do you mean, Rupert?'

'I would like to see you settled as mistress of Wootton Magna Hall, not so far from Max and Cecily and your grandmama.' Rupert spoke quietly and watched her face as he did so.

'You mean. . . ?' Makine could not complete the question but her heart was thumping.

'I asked you once before to be my wife, but your cousin was threatening to disgrace you. I have stayed quiet all this time, but my regard for you is the same. I would like you to become my wife, Maxine.'

Maxine looked at Rupert and knew that here was a person she could be happy with. There had been no mention of love – only regard – but she knew she was nearer to loving him than any other person she had ever met. Perhaps love was over for him, buried with his dear wife. She felt a strong tug of feeling but she knew it was not enough. I must love the person I marry, she told herself, and I do not want just regard however kindly it is said.

'Sir Rupert . . .' she started to say, but was stopped by his lips on hers. He had pulled her to her feet and into his arms; his lips were telling her things his words had denied. The kiss went on and Maxine surrendered; his fingers were on her throat, her shoulder, her breast until she trembled.

He lifted his head at last. 'You cannot say no, my sweet. Whatever tale your cousin spreads about your reputation, it means nothing to me. I know you to be the Maxine who would never have behaved improperly with such a man as George Lidiard. You cannot deny it.'

Maxine lifted her head bewildered. Just when she thought she knew her own heart, her own feelings, Rupert had remembered the threat of her disgrace at the hands of her cousin. She would not, could not bring that disgrace upon the Wootton family.

She stood proudly as she spoke to him. 'No, I cannot do it, Rupert. The shame would be too much. If we loved it might be different, but you speak only of your regard and I have the same regard for you. It is not enough to overcome the wickedness of my cousin. I will not embarrass you further. Max and I will move into Lidiard House with my cousin. You can be free of any rumours which George might spread and we can meet in society without embarrassment. I will leave you.'

Left on his own, Rupert was calling himself a fool and not for the first time, he thought.

I love her so much yet I have not dared to say it. As long as George Lidiard is on the scene, she will never listen if I speak of love. And he has the upper hand as long as he can tell of those years when Maxine, masquerading as her brother, lived with him in his home. If she but loved me, I think we could overcome it all, but how can I search for her love as long as she is threatened by her cousin? I could almost wish we could think of a scheme to give her some regard for me, just as those children did for Cecily. But I am too old for such pranks, he told himself ... then hesitated and gave a rueful grin. Perhaps I can ask Freddy. I will go and speak to him straight away.

Freddy was found together with Gareth and Jessica and as usual, he was making them laugh.

I am getting old, Rupert said to himself, I cannot laugh like that any more.

But he succeeded in detaching Freddy and drawing him into a quiet corner.

'I want your advice, Freddy,' Rupert said.

Freddy looked astonished. 'You want *my* advice, Sir Rupert? I had thought it to be more likely the other way round!'

'No, let me tell you my problem. I should be able to solve it myself but I seem to be making a hash of it.' And he told Freddy of his love for Maxine and the difficulties it had brought.

Freddy knew the story of Maxine's life with George Lidiard and could understand the problem. He instantly came up with a solution.

'Make her jealous,' he said.

Rupert stared. 'You mean. . . ?'

'Yes, make up to some other female and let Maxine know of it. I am sure she loves you, I have seen her looking at you, but she is afraid of George, you see. A rotter and a rake, her cousin, no other word for it. Disgrace to the name of Lidiard. Would be glad to pay him back for some of the unhappiness he has caused Maxine. Very fond of Maxine, you know.'

'Yes, I believe you, Freddy,' replied Rupert and he sounded dubious. 'And I can see your reasoning, but I do not know any other young ladies at the moment.'

'No trouble,' grinned Freddy. 'We'll get an actress.'

'Get an actress. . . ?' echoed Rupert as though he had not heard Freddy aright.

'Yes, easy. I know a nice girl. Good actress, will do anything to oblige for a couple of guineas, and I know you're not short of the blunt.'

Rupert put his hand an the young man's sleeve. 'Slow down, Freddy, slow down. Do you mean that I should make friends with this . . . er, actress . . . take her about in order to make Maxine jealous?'

'Yes, that's right, got the idea. Maxine sees you with someone else, realizes she loves you and nothing else matters. Will fall into your arms. She won't worry about any threat from her cousin once she knows you love her and she has you to protect her.' Freddy looked triumphant.

Rupert laughed. Then laughed again. 'Freddy, you are a genius. No wonder Jessica laughs at you so much. I think she is becoming rather fond of you.'

'I like Jessica; very nice girl, your daughter, Sir Rupert. Younger than me but knows how to go about things. Can I tell her the prank? She will help you know. She did with Cecily. No one else though, not even Max. Keep it to ourselves.'

'Freddy, what am I letting myself in for? I am not a youngster any more though still the right side of forty. I dare say I could enter into it if it means securing Maxine.'

'Bound to be a success, sir. I will see Suzanne, that is her name, Suzanne Maitland, though I don't think it is her proper name. She's a good girl. Will do whatever you tell her.' He looked at the older man. 'I think it would be best to pretend that she is the daughter of a cousin of yours from Leicestershire. She can stay in your house as a friend of Jessica's and it will be all right and dandy.'

Rupert was shaking his head. 'It does not sound right and dandy to me. I can see myself landing into trouble or becoming a laughing stock, I am not sure which.'

'Not a bit of it. Will have you down the aisle with Maxine in no time and George Lidiard can go off to Weymouth to the ladybird he keeps there.' Freddy looked pleased with himself.

'There is no knowing what you are going to say next,' said

Rupert drily. 'But I do think perhaps you are right. Can I leave the arrangements to you?'

'Of course, I will come and see you in a few days' time and bring the young lady with me.'

Freddy, full of his manipulating of affairs was quite startled a few minutes later to come across Maxine looking rather morose.

'You look blue-devilled, Maxine. What is causing all this?'

She was glad to talk to Freddy. He was still the dear friend who had brought Max home from the Peninsula.

'Marriage,' she said in an outright manner and never knew why she said it.

'Not about to be leg-shackled, are you?' replied Freddy knowing full well what the problem was.

'No, I am determined to be a good spinster and aunt to Max and Cecily's children. I shall enjoy that.'

'Fiddle,' he said. 'Can't have you talking like that, they ain't even wed yet. Wouldn't like to marry me, would you, Maxine? Am very fond of you and it would keep it all in the family as I said before . . . what is the matter?' he asked.

For Maxine was laughing. It was a reaction after the tensions of the evening and. who better to make her laugh than Freddy?

'Oh, Freddy, you are priceless beyond diamonds. I am laughing because that is the third offer of marriage I have received this evening. And I have turned down every one of them. It must be a record.'

'Do you mean you are turning me down?' he said with pretended offence. 'I am quite put out.'

'You are not put out at all,' she said cheerfully. 'You know very well you have your eyes set on Jessica when she is a little older.'

'Maybe, maybe not,' he replied smoothly. 'Would have married you had you accepted, Maxine. Don't like to see you downcast, you know.'

'I am not downcast any more, Freddy, you have cheered me up. Shall we stand up for the country dance?'

'I am supposed to ask you, ma'am!'

'Well, you ask me then and I will gladly accept.' And so the evening passed.

Freddy was as good as his word and just three days later, he announced himself at the Wootton house in Suffolk Square. He arrived in his curricle accompanied by a young lady who could only be described as fetching. He handed her down and picked up her portmanteau for her. She was dressed in a very deep blue pelisse and matching bonnet and, as she had fair curls, she made a pretty picture. She was introduced as Miss Suzanne Maitland and as Freddy had diplomatically sent a note to Sir Rupert purporting to come from his cousin in Leicestershire, she was ushered into the drawing-room where Rupert was sitting with Jessica.

Rupert did not know what to make of his feelings for he rather regretted the plan he had made with Freddy, but when he saw the young lady, he thought perhaps his task would be easy.

'Sir Rupert,' said Freddy jovially. 'I met your cousin's daughter as I promised and would like to introduce you. I know you are related but have not met before. Suzanne, this is Sir Rupert Wootton. Sir Rupert, Miss Suzanne Maitland. And I must not forget Jessica.' He smiled at the young girl who had been staring fascinated for she had been let into the secret and was determined to play her part. She loved Maxine and wanted to see her friend happy with her papa.

'Why, Jessica,' said Freddy quite seriously. 'You do look like cousins for you are both fair.'

Suzanne made a curtsy to Sir Rupert and then took off her bonnet. Rupert was pleased to see the sensible face of a girl whom he knew was older than Maxine, but who looked the same age as Jessica. Then she smiled at him and with her brilliant blue eyes, he was aware that she could be bewitching.

'Suzanne,' he said politely, 'I am pleased to welcome you to Suffolk Square and I hope your stay with us will be a happy one. Your mother is well?'

'Yes, quite well, thank you, Sir Rupert, and she sends her best regards to you.'

Rupert gave a sigh of relief. Her reply was nicely said and she seemed a prettily behaved young lady.

From that day on, Sir Rupert was to be seen nowhere without Jessica and Suzanne. He was also seen to be attentive to his young cousin and tongues wagged. He obtained vouchers for Almack's and waltzed with her there; he took her riding in the Park; and a select ball was held at Suffolk Square in her honour. Rupert even found an elderly aunt to play hostess and welcome his guests.

Maxine was not slow to notice all this. Now at Lidiard House with Max and George, she found that she missed Rupert more than she would have believed possible. She could not complain of George's behaviour as he insisted on taking her about when Max was visiting Cecily. Sometimes they made a foursome and gradually, Maxine became aware of a change in George.

He did not drink so much; he visited the gambling hells less than he had been used to do, and most surprising of all, he was quiet and pleasant to her. She did not like him any the more for he seemed elderly to her, but she was glad of his escort now that Sir Rupert had dropped out of the picture.

But Max was suspicious. 'Watch Cousin George, Maxine,' he said one morning when they were on their own. 'I think he is playing a deep game. It is not in his nature to be polite and amusing; I believe it to be a ploy to obtain you as a wife and his hands on your share of the de Rochefort fortune.'

'I do not think you are right, Max; you do him an injustice.' Maxine never thought the day would have come when she jumped to her cousin's defence. 'Since we have moved in with him, I have not been able to fault his behaviour and I did not expect ever to be able to say that.'

'And what do you think of the new arrival in Suffolk Square? Pretty, is she not? Rupert seems quite taken with her.'

Maxine was silent. She had been introduced to Suzanne and did think her pretty in an insipid kind of way. She was surprised to find Rupert taken with that style of looks, but she had to credit Suzanne with good behaviour and a compliant nature. Perhaps that is what Rupert needs for his peace of mind, she would say to herself.

'You are quiet, Maxine.'

She nodded. 'Yes, I know. I cannot fault Suzanne and she and Jessica have become bosom bows. I wonder how long she stays at Suffolk Square?'

'Perhaps she is out to catch Rupert and make it a permanent home. You were slow there, Maxine; I was sure Sir Rupert was going to offer for you. I suppose our cousin was the obstacle.'

Again, Maxine was silent. She felt that she had a lot of thinking to do and she was unsure both of her thoughts and her feelings – feelings that were both uncertain and turbulent and which came to a head on the evening of the party in honour of Sir Rupert's cousin.

TWELVE

$\mathcal{A}$LTHOUGH THE SUFFOLK Square residence had no ballroom as at Courtney House, there was space in the drawing-room for about ten couples and the young people were enjoying themselves at the party given for Suzanne.

George, Max and Maxine had arrived together and for almost the first time, Maxine was glad of her cousin's escort. His attire was modest and formal, only the elaborate neck-cloth showing any indication of his previous flamboyance.

Rupert was standing with a rather formidable lady who was one of his Wootton aunts, the young Suzanne at their side. Max looked at the guest carefully and could not fault her. She was remarkably like Jessica, but a slender and graceful height replaced Rupert's young daughter's tomboyish little figure which so attracted Freddy.

Suzanne was wearing a gown of a creamy-gold, almost the colour of her hair, the low bodice being embroidered exquisitely in fine knots. As Maxine watched her greet the guests, she was struck by her grace and poise and could not but notice that in between greeting the guests, she would look up at Rupert and then say something to make him smile.

He looks happy, decided Maxine, and he looks younger. I must admire her, indeed it is impossible to fault her, but does it mean I have lost Rupert? It is silly of me to say or think that; Rupert gave me my chance and I turned him down. Twice he has asked me to marry him and I turned him down each time. Now I am watching the consequences, but I will not show any jealousy ... the word startled her. Am I jealous? Jealousy implies that I care that Rupert is seeking a wife elsewhere. I should be happy for him but I am not ... oh, fiddle, I do not seem to know my own feelings. I must forget Rupert Wootton and his professed regard for me.

Then she found herself with George and Rupert, the pretty Suzanne standing with her hand on Rupert's arm.

'Pleased you could come, Lidiard,' said Rupert pleasantly. 'Have you managed to persuade Maxine to marry you yet?'

Maxine stiffened. Whatever possessed Rupert to say such a thing? He knew very well her feelings for her cousin.

But George was replying. Maxine listened with horror and Suzanne with interest. 'Give me time, Wootton; I hope to be able to make an announcement soon.' And George looked at Rupert's companion. 'Miss Maitland, you seem to be making a certain gentleman very happy and I wish you success. May I steal you for a moment? Will you stand up for the quadrille with me?'

Suzanne accepted gracefully and Maxine was left with a smiling Rupert. She felt as though her heart had been squeezed and she had no feelings except those of a hard bitterness.

'Maxine, do you not think Suzanne to be a very pretty young lady?'

'She is delightful, Rupert,' Maxine replied, and she thought her tone was icy. 'Is it too soon to offer my congratulations?'

He sat down at her side. 'I must say I have been agreeably surprised. When my cousin wrote to ask me if her daughter could spend a few weeks with us, I thought it seemed rather an imposition. She knows very well that I have no wife to act as chaperon and I have to rely on Elsie. But from the start, it has proved a very successful visit, partly, I suppose, because Suzanne and Jessica have become such good friends.' He paused and looked at her, fully aware of his perfidy and hoping that Freddy's plan would bear fruit. Certainly Maxine looked anything but happy at that moment. 'I am sorry I worried you with my attentions, Maxine. You will be better off with George; he seems quite hopeful.'

'I am sure I do not know why. I have said nothing to him to indicate that I am going to change my mind. It did not take long to change yours, Rupert.' The words were bluntly said and Maxine was appalled at herself.

'You made me realize that my case was hopeless. There were too many things from the past to stand between us, Maxine.'

You rat, Rupert, he was saying to himself, but then added fuel to the fire, 'You will feel more comfortable with your cousin.'

'You think so?' she asked him tartly.

'I am sure so. To have acted the highwayman has put you beyond the pale. Only George knows the real truth of the matter, apart from myself, that is.' Rupert had never felt so false, but he had promised Freddy to try and pick a quarrel with Maxine.

'You will be much better suited with your fair-haired cousin, Rupert,' Maxine observed.

'I think maybe I will and for that I will be grateful to you for turning me down.'

'I never thought to hear you say that, sir.'

'No, I quite thought I was being correct in giving you the protection of my name.' Have I gone far enough, thought Rupert, she is not really angry. 'But Suzanne coming to London seems to have changed all that.'

'So you never did love me?' Maxine shot the words as from a gun and knew it was the most foolish thing she had ever said, but she could feel the anger boiling up inside of her.

181

'Love?' Rupert succeeded in looking supercilious. 'I do not think that love ever entered into the matter. It would have been very much a marriage of convenience.'

'Rupert Wootton!' Maxine exploded at last. 'You have the effrontery to offer for me twice and then to say it would have been a marriage of convenience. Was it supposed to be convenient for me – a masquerader, a gentleman of the road – to be given the Wootton name to make me respectable? You can keep your respectability, Sir Rupert, that is not what I look for in a marriage. I look for love, and I know now that I would never have found it with you. Here is your dear Suzanne. Take her and dance the waltz with her. Waltz her out of my life for I hope that now that Max and I have removed to Lidiard House, I will not need to acknowlededae your acquaintance again.'

Her voice had risen and she knew she was being shrewish but she did not care. She looked at George, now standing at her side. 'There you are, George, please take me home for I have the headache. It is unbearably hot in here.'

And without giving the stunned Rupert a chance to speak again, she swept out of the room on George's arm.

Rupert led Suzanne to his aunt and hastily went in search of Freddy, who, as usual was with Gareth and Jessica.

'Freddy, I must talk to you. I have quarrelled with Maxine.'

'You have sir?' Freddy was all admiration. 'Did she lose her temper with you?'

'Worse than that. I was treated to a tirade and she has gone home with George. I feel as though I have ruined my chances for ever. . . .'

'Not a bit of it, sir. If she has lost her temper then you can be certain that she loves you. We are nearly there.' Freddy was smiling.

'I am not smiling, Freddy, I feel as though I have cooked my goose completely.'

'We'll soon have a turn around, Sir Rupert. Suzanne is acting very pretty, is she not?'

'Very pretty indeed,' said Ruper gloomily. 'She has scarcely a single word of intelligent conversation.'

'She looks the part, dammit, you cannot deny it.'

'No, I am not denying it, but I shall be glad to see the last of her. I had better go and ask her for the country dance.' He moved away and Freddy made his parting shot.

'Not long now, Sir Rupert, you trust me.'

Maxine having put on her pelisse in the cool evening air, sat gloomily beside George in his carriage.

'Nice little girl that Suzanne of Wootton's. I wonder if she will snap him up. About time he married again.'

'Yes, I suppose so.'

'Thought he was looking to you at one time, Maxine, but I expect the scandal attaching to your name has made him look else-where.'

'Be quiet, George,' Maxine snapped.

'Sorry, Cousin, you not feeling quite the thing?'

'No, I am not,' she snapped again.

And at Lidiard House, she reached the sanctuary of her bedroom, flung herself on the bed and burst into tears. It is my own fault, she said into her pillow. I refused him twice and now I have lost him. Oh, Rupert, I love you. I know it now and it is too late. You have the pretty Suzanne, and I hate her. I am jealous, Rupert, eaten up with jealousy. And I am a fool. Yet how could I accept your offer when you spoke only of your regard? It was love I sought. Love would have overcome all the embarrassments of the past, I know it now. And I am sure you would have come to love me in time.

She sat up and took off her pelisse. Now I am left with Cousin George; he has been kind of late but I cannot trust him. Yet if I married him, I would be near Grandmama and Max and Cecily. Is it possible to marry for such a reason? I almost wish I had an oracle who would tell me, she thought foolishly. And smiling at herself, she got ready for bed and much to her surprise, she slept soundly.

All the following week, Maxine let George escort her to Almack's and ride in the park with her. She managed to avoid Rupert and was, at the same time, glad and heartbroken. She was certain of only one thing: she could never marry anyone else – certainly not her Cousin George – as long as she felt this love for Rupert. She had thought that perhaps her feelings would abate as the days passed, but time was to be no healer for Maxine.

By the end of the following week, she noticed that George seemed fidgety. She could not explain it. He had behaved himself very properly so she wondered if his gaming debts had caught up with him.

He took her one evening to Vauxhall Gardens where there was to be a ridotto and a show of fireworks. The pleasure gardens were very popular as an evening's entertainment; wine flowed and there was dancing in the rotunda.

Maxine had always wanted to visit the gardens, having heard various dubious tales about the entertainment there.

It astonished her just how many people George Lidiard knew. As they watched the dancers, she was made aware that some of his acquaintances were what she could only describe as vulgar and that more than one painted female with ridiculously high feathered head-dresses stopped to speak to him, even daring to give him a kiss.

'You have a lot of acquaintances, George.' she said at last.

'Oh, Vauxhall Gardens is one of my favourite haunts. Always fun and games here, most entertaining,' he replied glibly.

'Even the painted ladies?' she asked caustically.

'They know George Lidiard is good for a game of faro and doesn't mind parting with a guinea or two.'

And Maxine was jerked into the past and across England into Dorset. This was the real George, the one she had disliked so much. Plenty of money for his own pleasures, but none to spare for those dependent on him. I must not forget it, she was saying to herself, as she watched him put his arm around a female of uncertain years who could never be described as a lady.

Forget the thoughtful George of the weeks since the quarrel with Rupert. This was the real George and one to be avoided. Then she realized that the doxy of a woman was addressing her.

'So you're snapping up our George, are you? We shall miss him, but he needs to be setting up his nursery or it will be too late.' These words were followed by a raucous laugh which made Maxine wince, but with which George joined in.

And Maxine felt his arm go round her. 'Yes, this is my Maxine, hopefully Mrs George Lidiard in the not too distant future.'

'Good luck, miss, you'd better put him on leading-reins, I'm thinking.' And with another laugh, she moved off.

'Who was that?' Maxine asked faintly.

'That was Dolly, a good sort Dolly. Never short of a laugh when you're with Dolly.'

'She is very vulgar, George.'

He looked down and saw that her face was serious but it did not seem to warn him. 'Oh yes, she is vulgar all right, but no harm in her. Shall have to give her up when we are married, Maxine.'

She looked up quickly. 'What did you say?'

'Hoping we can be married soon, Maxine, can't put it off much longer if I want an heir. And we've been dealing very well these last weeks since you left the respectable Sir Rupert behind.'

Maxine froze. Rupert? George? She loved one and hated the other. She knew it very forcibly in that crowded noisy pavilion at Vauxhall Gardens.

George seemed not to notice her forbidding expression. 'How

about naming the day, my dear? And how about a kiss? Haven't had a kiss for a long time and this jolly place always puts me in a kissing mood.'

And he turned her to him and kissed her ruthlessly until she managed to struggle free. 'Very nice, Maxine. And now about our wedding day. The first day of next month, would that give you enough time to find a dress and all the trappings? Not prepared to wait a lot longer for you. Have been very patient, you must admit.'

Maxine thought she felt sick but she swallowed hard and prepared herself to give her reply.

'George, I am never going to marry you,' she said stonily.

'What's that? Never? No such word, Maxine. You have no choice, damn you. I need your money and you know quite well that I'll spread the tale of your indiscretions if you don't marry me. No one will touch you.' George was his old blustering self.

'I have told you before that I would rather remain a spinster for the rest of my life than be married to you. I mean it.'

'My dear girl, we can't have that, I will think about it.'

'There is no need. That is my final word. You can take me home.'

Afterwards, Maxine thought that the disastrous conversation and its outcome must have been the result of George being in his cups. He returned the very next morning to his civil and kind attention to her needs and took her wherever she wished to go. She forced herself to put the ugly incident at Vauxhall Gardens out of her mind.

The weeks slid into spring and Maxine became accustomed to seeing Rupert in the company of Miss Suzanne Maitland. No declaration was forthcoming, but neither did Suzanne show any sign of returning to Leicestershire. Maxine's heartbreak did not become any the less; she felt as though she had sustained a great loss in her life.

In the middle of the first week of April with the cold winds of

March behind them and blossom showing on the trees in the London squares, George sought Maxine at Lidiard House in the early afternoon. She was sitting in the drawing-room absorbed in one of Mrs Edgeworth's tales. She had read it before but she always found it amusing.

'There you are, Maxine,' said George cheerily as he entered the room. 'The most surprising thing. I have been looking at a book of old London churches and guess what I have found?'

'Old London churches does not sound like you, George.' Maxine replied with good humour.

'You do not know me, Cousin, even after all these years. It seems there is a church out at Kew which has a tomb inside belonging to someone of the family of Lidiard. Would you believe it? I thought all the Lidiards were in Dorset. I would very much like to see it. What do you think of having a trip out there? We could go in the curricle. It is not very far and the weather is turning warmer now.'

Maxine looked at her cousin. He seemed quite serious and it would certainly be interesting to see a Lidiard tomb. 'I think I would like it, George; when would you wish to go?'

'There is no rush. What about this coming Saturday morning if the weather is fine? If it is wet then we could make the visit sometime next week. Might as well choose a good day, you know.'

'Yes, certainly, I will look forward to it.'

Saturday morning came and it being fine, George insisted on being on the road by ten o'clock. They could have a nuncheon in a tavern at Kew, he said.

Maxine was pleased and dressed herself in one of her better pelisses, a dark cream with a trim of navy-blue velvet. Her bonnet was also cream and George remarked on her appearance as he handed her up on to the curricle at the front of Lidiard House.

'You do me proud, Maxine, my word you do.'

Maxine smiled; George was known to be fulsome with his compliments. He himself was dressed to a fault and in grey with white knee-breeches. His top coat was also grey with only four capes which was very modest for George.

Once out of London, the traffic was light and he chatted pleasantly to her. His pair of chestnuts were neat steppers and he handled them lightly.

The church was easily found and George secured a boy to look to his horses' heads.

The church door creaked and George held it open for Maxine. She stepped inside to a rather dark church although there were lighted candles at the altar.

'Where shall we start looking, George?' she asked quietly.

'Just a moment, Maxine, a little business to conduct first,' he said evenly.

'Whatever do you mean?' Even as she said the words, a clergyman stepped out of what seemed to be the vestry and started walking towards them.

'Mr Lidiard, welcome. And this is Miss Rochefort? Splendid.' The words from the priest were quiet but assured and Maxine imagined that George had arranged with the parson to show them the tomb.

It was when she saw two people who were sitting in the front pew rise to their feet and she felt the grip of George's hand on her arm, that Maxine knew that there was something very wrong indeed.

She stopped still at the chancel steps and George stood quietly by her side. Even as she heard the parson's first words, she did not guess what was happening.

'Dearly beloved, we are gathered together here in the sight of God. . . .'

'George,' she hissed suddenly and with a note of panic. 'What have you done?'

'Hush, just arranged for us to be wed. Thought you would like it.'

Blind fury assailed Maxine. She ignored the falter in the parson's voice, tore her arm from George's grasp and turned and ran as fast as she could, banging the church door behind her and flying in the direction of the curricle. She snatched the reins from the boy's hands and shouted at him. 'The gentleman wants you, he'll give you a guinea.'

She clambered up on to the seat, reins in her hands and set off. Before she had gone more than a few yards, she heard a commotion coming from the church and the sound of her name from an enraged George.

Maxine had not been George Lidiard's steward for five years for nothing. She had driven his curricle to Dorchester or Weymouth with ease and a confident flick of the whip. Now she concentrated on getting through the traffic in Kew before she reached the turnpike road which led into London.

It was only then that she seemed to breathe at all and her thoughts caught up with her actions. She had driven all that way in a furious rage and could not remember seeing any other vehicle or cattle on the road at all.

She did not know who she was the more angry with; herself at being taken in by a smooth, lying George, or with George himself for daring to get her into a church in order to marry her. I'll never forgive him. I'll never even see him again if I can help it. Lidiard tombstone indeed. It is George who should be lying beneath a Lidiard tombstone.

All that easy friendship once I had quarrelled with Rupert. I should have been warned. Max did try to tell me. How can I possibly have been so easily duped? Though now I come to think of it I did question his reading a book of London churches. But still I saw no danger.

189

By now, she was along the Chiswick High Road and into Hammersmith and she had to concentrate on her horses, forget the past hour and decide what to do with the immediate future.

She gained Lidiard House and took the curricle round to the stables not saying a word to a gaping stable boy. Then luck was on her side, for she passed no servant and she could hear cook busy in the kitchen. She guessed that Max had gone to Courtney House.

Upstairs, she stood still for one second then made up her mind. I will go to Grandmama but I will tell no one. She flung off her clothes and with a decision she did not consciously make, dressed herself in one of her gentleman's coats and breeches which she had kept folded up in a drawer as a reminder of the time she had dressed as a boy.

I will have to travel on the stage, she was muttering aloud. It will be easier if I am a gentleman. Oh my goodness, my hair . . . and she quickly found scissors and cut off some of the forward ringlets and tied the longer back hair into a knot with ribbon. It will have to pass, she thought. A lot of young men wear their hair longer these days. Boots she found and a neck-cloth which she tied in the simplest fall that she knew.

Wait, wait, something seemed to tell her. You will need dresses once you get to Lidiard Grange, and she flew into a spare room and came back with a small portmanteau. She carefully packed three dresses, a light pelisse and some pumps. Anything else she would have to borrow from Cousin Rose.

Then another problem hit her. Money. How much will I need for the stage? She had no idea. Not deterred, she ran out of the room again and into Max's bedroom where she knew he kept spare bank notes. Oh goodness, was her next thought, I cannot carry a reticule. Max, I'll have to borrow one of your top coats and put the bank notes in the pocket.

Anything else? she asked herself. She knew she must waste no time for George would be hot on her heels once he had found a conveyance.

A note for Max. It is only fair. And she sat at his small writing table and found pen and ink and a piece of paper. She wrote hurriedly.

Dear Max

George tried to make me marry him - cannot go into details. I have run away. I have gone by stage and have taken some of your money. Do not look for me and do not worry about me. I have gone dressed as a young man so it should be all right.

Love Maxine

A last look round and she made her escape from the house, but thought that everything was lost when she bumped into Mrs Prebble the cook who was coming out of the kitchen.

'My word, Master Max, you are in a hurry.'

Saved again, thought Maxine. 'Promised to meet Cecily. Late already, Mrs Prebble,' she replied keeping her voice as low as she could.

She knew where the West Country stage went from but not the times it left. She had missed the early morning stage but thought that there would probably be one at midday. It was now nearly twelve o'clock. And she was in luck once again. There was no seat on the coach to be had, but one place left on the top and she did not mind this. She paid her fare, climbed up and sat down thankfully.

THIRTEEN

$\mathcal{M}$AXINE ENJOYED HER journey into Dorset. The stage-coach made slow progress out of London, but once on the turnpike roads, they were able to travel more quickly.

Her companions on top of the coach were all male and all jolly. Their wives and children travelled inside and more than once, Maxine felt thankful for her hasty decision to travel as a young man.

There were many halts on the way, but the coaching-inns were clean and respectable, if simple.

Maxine would have been happier in her mind if she had not had the worries of her future life to plague her. She had cast off Sir Rupert Wootton and all the comfort and care he would have had to offer; she had fled from Cousin George. The only amusement she had on the journey was to think of him at the church door in Kew, calling her name in vain and watching his curricle disappearing down the main street.

At last, they arrived in Sherborne, but as the stage was travelling on to Yeovil, the driver obliged her by saying he would set her down at the end of the lane that led to Nether Compton. As Lidiard Grange was situated just outside the village and only a mile from the turnpike road, she did not have far to walk.

She approached the old house with some trepidation, but then decided to walk straight in unannounced, hoping to find her grandmother in the drawring-room. If Cousin Rose was with her, it could not be helped.

But the Dowager Countess Hampton was on her own and as Rose was on a visit to Lidiard Manor, she was feeling bored and restless.

When the door opened and she saw the young man standing there, she gave a beaming smile.

'Max! And where have you sprung from?' And she rose from her chair and approached the unexpected visitor. She gave a gasp of astonishment as she did so. 'Blue eyes. It is Maxine, I declare. Well, miss, what are you doing here and up to your old tricks dressed just like your brother? Who are you trying to hoax this time? Come and sit down and tell me. We are on our own as Rose has gone on a visit to Lidiard Manor.'

Maxine kissed her grandmother's cheek. 'Grandmama, I have brought some dresses with me. Would you prefer me to change out of my coat and breeches? I think they are weary from travelling on the stage, in any case.'

The exclamation from the dowager was of mock horror. 'Travelling on the stage? You do not mean to tell me you have travelled from London on the stage! Whatever will you do next? And what has become of George, and where is Sir Rupert Wootton in all this?'

'It is a long story, Grandmama.'

'Well, you go up to a guest room and get yourself changed and looking like Maxine again and I will order a tray of tea. I was feeling bored on my own; your story will divert me.'

'I think it will horrify you rather than divert you,' said Maxine with a smile.

'Away with you, young lady. I do not think that anything can be more horrifying than you living with George all those years masquerading as your brother.'

The story took a long time in the telling, but the dowager listened attentively and made only one or two interruptions.

'Well, Maxine, a good pair you have chosen to associate with. George is a fool, I have always known it. I have no doubt he has gone chasing down to Weymouth to be comforted by his *chère amie*. As for Sir Rupert, I credited him with more sense. He should have snapped you up whatever your reply to him might have been; none of this giving his attention to his young cousin. Whatever is the man thinking of? I vow he will come running after you.'

But Maxine was shaking her head. 'No, you are wrong, Grandmama. We quarrelled and it is not fair to expect him to make me his wife. My reputation is tarnished and it would not do for the wife of Sir Rupert Wootton.'

'Balderdash,' exclaimed the elderly lady. 'There are scandals in every family. He will know that you behaved properly when you were with your cousin. George can spread as many tales as he likes. No one will believe him.'

'I wish I could think so, Grandmama,' said Maxine sadly.

They would both have been interested and amused if they had been able to see through the windows of Lidiard House and Sir Rupert's home in Suffolk Square.

It had taken an infuriated George Lidiard an hour to procure a conveyance to take him from Kew to London and he was not in the best of tempers when he arrived at Lidiard House.

Then he could only find Cook. 'Miss Maxine? No, Mr Lidiard, I have seen nothing of her. Only Mr Max, he was leaving with a portmanteau, late this morning it was.'

'Are you sure it was Mr Max?'

Mrs Prebble stared. 'I do not wish to be impertinent, sir, but I can tell the difference between a young lady and a young gentleman.'

It told George nothing, and it was not until Max arrived home that he was able to discover the truth. Max had come in, found Maxine's note and gone hastily in search of his cousin. He found George with a decanter of sherry in front of him in the library.

'George, what in damnation is all this?' Max said. He was waving Maxine's note. 'Maxine says that you tried to force her to marry you and she has run away. Gone dressed as a young man again, as well. What do you know about it?'

For once in his life, George Lidiard seemed humbled. 'Wanted Maxine for a wife,' he said gloomily. 'She wouldn't have me so I tricked her and got her in front of a parson. Then, damme, if she didn't run off and took my curricle with her. Left me standing and feeling a fool. When I got back here, the curricle was round in the stables and no sign of Maxine. Thought she might have gone to Wootton's place in Suffolk Square, but I dare not go and ask.' He looked up. 'She wouldn't say she had run away if she had gone there, would she? It is my idea that she loves the fellow and here he is taken up with this chit of a cousin of his. So where do you suppose Maxine is?'

Max was thoughtful. 'I think she would go to our grandmother's.'

'But how would she get there? It is miles into Dorset.'

'Probably went on the stage; she took some of my money,' replied Max.

'On the stage? Maxine? Whatever will the girl do next? Oh, but you said she had dressed as a young man, I suppose that would not be quite so scandalous. Tell you what, Max, she's too much for me. Playing the highwayman and all that. Think I will get myself down to Weymouth and set up house with my Diana. She's a good girl, though past being a girl. I will let out Triscombe House. Don't want a house for you and Cecily, do you, Max? Oh no, of course, you are going to have Lidiard Grange, be damned to it, ought to have been mine. Nothing seems to go right. I'll go down to Weymouth in the carriage, you can have the use of the curricle if you want it and stay on here as long as you wish. Have come by my deserts, have I not, Max? Need a while with Diana to recover. . . .'

And Max left George grumbling to himself and went back to his room to consider what to do next about Maxine. I think a visit to Sir Rupert is called for, he decided. I had better take Freddy with me, time this charade was finished.

Although Freddy's plan with the actress had been known only by Jessica, Max had learned of it only a few days before. Going the round of the clubs with Freddy, he had learned the whole story. This from a Freddy who was slightly foxed and disappointed that the affair had not been so far resolved. He had been glad to talk to Max about it but had made Max promise to say nothing to his sister.

That fateful morning, Max had already called on Cecily at Courtney House, but after a nuncheon, he returned and found Freddy there. He told him the latest development in the saga that Freddy had initiated.

'That's done the trick,' Freddy said. 'The dear girl will be bereft. Best thing is for Sir Rupert to go chasing after her.'

'But what about Suzanne?'

'Don't worry. I will see to Suzanne. She's played her part and has done very well. I will pay her and she can go back to being an actress on the stage.' He looked at the worried Max. 'Shall we both go and see Sir Rupert?'

All the Woottons and Suzanne were out when they arrived at Suffolk Square, but the two young men made themselves comfortable in the drawing-room and waited.

When Jessica and Suzanne came bursting in with Sir Rupert behind them, they knew instantly by the expression on the faces of Max and Freddy that something was afoot.

Sir Rupert, weary of the clinging Miss Maitland, and regretting his quarrel with Maxine, spoke directly to Freddy. 'You had better come into the library. There is something I wish to discuss with you. Bring Max with you. Did you wish to see me especially?'

'It is rather urgent, Sir Rupert,' replied Max.

In the library, Rupert poured them all some brandy and asked them what the trouble was.

'Maxine has run away,' said her brother.

Rupert was startled. 'She cannot have run away, she is living in George Lidiard's pocket.'

And he was told what had happened that morning. He looked grave.

'Poor little girl,' he said.

Freddy and Max looked at each other in some amusement at the thought of Maxine being described as 'a poor little girl'.

Rupert was looking at Freddy. 'You got me into this tangle, Freddy, what have you to suggest now?'

Freddy smiled broadly. 'End in sight,' he said. 'Happy ending, too. I pay Suzanne off; you go down to Wootton Magna – pretty sure Maxine will have gone to her grandmother at Nether Compton, that's so, ain't it, Max? As soon as you hear she has arrived at Lidiard Grange, you can go over and claim her. Has been obvious for weeks that she is jealous of Suzanne, stands to reason it is you she loves if she has run away from George.'

Rupert stepped forward and shook hands with Freddy. 'Have to thank you, Freddy, I think it is going to be all right. I will go staight into Dorset and wait for Maxine to arrive. And, Freddy, please look after Jessica for me while I am away. I do not think you will find that difficult and if in a year's time, you are still of the same mind, I cannot say that I will not welcome you as a son-in-law.

Freddy beamed.

At Lidiard Grange, both the dowager and Maxine were doing a lot of thinking. But neither told the other their thoughts: so Maxine brooded and her grandmother acted.

The dowager was by now certain that Sir Rupert Wootton and her granddaughter loved each other. She was suspicious about the account of Sir Rupert's behaviour with his young visitor. She might be as pretty as Maxine made her out to be, but she did not sound in the least suitable to be the next mistress of Wootton Magna Hall. From what Maxine had said, the young lady seemed to be no older than his own children. No, decided Lady Lidiard, he probably made up to the girl in order to make Maxine jealous and he has succeeded. It is my conviction that as soon he realizes that Maxine has run away from George, he will travel directly to Wootton Magna. He will guess that Lidiard Grange is the only place where the girl would find a welcome.

In fact, the dowager said to herself, working out the journey time of the slow stage-coach and the faster travelling time of Sir Rupert's carriage, he is quite likely already at his home. I will take the risk and send a boy over with a note.

Dear Sir Rupert

I think you will be pleased to know that my grand-daughter is staying with me at Lidiard Grange. I cannot be sure that she will be pleased to see you in view of the quarrel she has told me of, but you are welcome, to call here at any time.

Yours sincerely

Georgiana, Dowager Countess Hampton

Not knowing that her grandmother had done this, Maxine spent a miserable day after her arrival at Lidiard Grange. True, she had foiled George and she thought it unlikely he would renew his attentions. But she had also lost the man she loved. He was taken up with his young cousin and she could not blame him for she was a charming girl; he had been glad to turn to Suzanne after the bitter quarrel. I have brought it all on myself, thought Maxine. I could almost wish myself back in the saddle as Cousin George's steward. Looking back, they seemed to be happy, hard-working days with few problems except the squeezing of money out of her cousin for his tenants. Now what am I to do? I can hardly make my home with Grandmama if Max and Cecily are going to be living here. I suppose the truth is that I should have accepted Sir Rupert's 'regard' and hidden my love from him for ever.

When Sir Rupert drove over to Lidiard Grange in his curricle early next morning, Maxine happened to be standing at the window of the drawing-room. She was wondering what to do with the day and could not believe it when she saw the two horses driven swiftly up the drive and recognized the horseman.

She ran to the front door as Rupert jumped down from the curricle, his expression inscrutable.

I don't want to see him, Maxine was thinking furiously, we will only quarrel again. How did he know I was here, in any case? He has probably come to visit Grandmama.

She was out of the front door and hurrying round to the rear of the house. She shouted at the same time, 'I do not want to see you. Grandmama is in the breakfast-room.'

And Rupert watched her disappear and gave a smile. He let himself into the house and made his way to the breakfast-room unannounced.

The dowager looked up, and then smiled. 'You lost no time, Sir Rupert. I assume that you received my message.'

'Thank you, Lady Lidiard, I did. Maxine saw me arrive and has run off saying that she does not wish to see me.'

'Silly girl. Go down through the kitchen into the back garden. You will see a small walled garden. It is meant for peaches, but I have yet to see any. There is a seat for my use; I like it there because it is sheltered and private. Maxine likes it, too, and you are sure to find her there. She will have guessed that I have told you to look for her there, and it will have given her time to gather her arguments against you. Do not waste any more time talking to me. And make sure of her this time.'

Rupert bent and kissed her lined forehead. They both smiled. 'Thank you,' was all he said.

In the walled garden, where Maxine was indeed sitting and expecting Rupert to arrive at any moment, she was doing exactly what her grandmother had predicted. He knows I am not fit to be his bride; I will tell him to go back to his frippery cousin, she was telling herself.

But when he opened the tall, wrought-iron gate and walked towards her, she felt as though her heart had missed a beat. How can I argue with him when I seem to have turned to a jelly, she thought.

'How did you know I was in Dorset?' she asked him before he had even time to greet her.

'Freddy and Max and I put our heads together and decided that this was your only refuge. I travelled down to Wootton Magna the next day and have been waiting for the word I was sure your grandmother would send me.'

'Grandmama wrote to you?' she asked stiffly.

'She did indeed; she is a redoubtable old lady.'

'I know that, but she should have consulted me. I do not wish to see you.' Maxine was looking up at him, their eyes clashed.

'May I sit down with you, Maxine?' he asked politely.

'No, you may not. You will put your arms around me and try to kiss me. I have a lot to say to you.' She was snappish.

'Very well,' he said with a smile. 'I am quite happy to stand and look at you. And you have come out without a wrap and it is not exactly summer yet.'

'Fustian. I am not cold. Did you know of the trick my despicable cousin played on me?'

'Yes, Max told me the gist of it. He came straight to me after speaking to George.'

'Max lost no time in coming to you. I left him a note to tell him not to worry about me. And what has Fredddy to do with it all?'

'Everything.'

She looked at him suspiciously. 'Everything? What are you talking about? He asked me to marry him not an hour after you had done the same—'

'What a lot of offers you have had, my dear.'

'I am not your "dear",' she said. 'Freddy's was the third that day and I refused all of them.'

'A very popular young lady,' he said with smooth irony.

'You are being insulting. Now will you please listen: I am not going to marry George; I hope never to see him again. Then I did not take Freddy seriously though it was kind of him to ask me. As for you, I quite expected an announcement of your betrothal to Suzanne. Is she here with you? No doubt she is content for the regard you have for her. Regard is not enough for me.'

Rupert said nothing. He knew his time had come. He sat on the wooden seat, his fingers tightly spanned her waist and he pulled her towards him totally ignoring her attempts to struggle.

His lips lingered on her breast and her throat before they found her lips, and Maxine was lost.

All the frustration and fury and jealousy she had felt were lost in a haze of sensation. He demanded her kiss with his lips while his fingers sought the soft skin below the bodice of her dress. She gave a gasp and jerked away from him.

'You cannot, you cannot—'

'Yes, I can. If my regard is not enough for you, will my love do instead?'

'You cannot love a young lady with a past as sullied as mine.'

'I adore her.'

'Rupert, what are you saying?' she asked hoarsely, her body still throbbing from his caress.

'I adore you. I love you. I have the greatest regard for you. I want to rush you to the altar just as George did. . . .'

'You dare mention my cousin George?'

'I will mention him. We will talk and laugh about George many times when we are man and wife. You will marry me, Maxine? Must I say it formally? Will you do me the honour of becoming my wife? And another question I have not yet asked of you though I knew my answer when I kissed you.'

Maxine knew herself beaten. She could not say no. 'I love you, Rupert, I know it now.'

'Only now?' he teased her.

She laughed at him then. 'I knew I loved you when you began taking notice of your Suzanne. I was jealous, Rupert.'

'Freddy said you would be.'

'Freddy?' she asked. 'That is the second time Freddy has come into the story. What has he to do with it all?'

'Everything.'

'Everything? That is what you said before. I do believe you are trying to make me cross. How can Freddy have influenced you?' she asked with a genuine curiosity.

'He introduced me to Suzanne.'

Maxine stood up. 'You are talking nonsense. Suzanne is your cousin's daughter. You told me so.'

'Lying, Maxine.'

'You were lying, Rupert? I do not believe it—' She was stopped in mid-sentence as Rupert pulled her back on to the seat and let his fingers ease the little puff sleeves of her dress from her shoulders until her bodice was nearly low enough to be indecent. 'You cannot do that, Rupert, we may be alone in the walled garden, but it is not proper in a young lady to behave in such a way.'

'You never were a very proper young lady, far from it. And I would like to see the whole of you, but had better wait until we are married. You are very beautiful.'

'You are trying to confuse me with words when I am now attempting to be the model of propriety. And if you do not tell me all this about Freddy and lying, I shall walk away.'

'You cannot walk anywhere with your dress in that state of disarray.'

'Rupert!' Maxine laughed and pretend exasperation, but she was sure of his love now. 'Tell me everything. What is all this about Suzanne and Freddy?'

'She is not my cousin at all. She an actress. Clever little girl; acted the part beautifully. She took you in, Maxine.'

Maxine stared at him and then spoke slowly. 'Do you mean you got an actress to play the part so that it would make me jealous?'

'Yes, that is right. It was Freddy's idea, he found Suzanne for me. He said it would make you realize that you loved me. He was right, Maxine?'

Maxine laughed then and flung her arms around Rupert's neck. She felt that she had never laughed like that in her whole life. 'I was *so* jealous and then I knew there was no one else for me but you, Rupert.' They kissed quickly. 'But, Rupert, I will say this for the very last time: what about those years I spent as a young man with only George for company, what about the highwayman? I do love you but I could not marry you with all that on my conscience.'

'Maxine, what happened in those years is only known by a handful of people. And George will not say anything because of his humiliation when you ran away from him – I must hear the whole story of that, by the way; even Max did not know exactly what had happened.' He held her close. 'I fell in love with a young highwayman who hid a female breast under his jacket. It took courage to do what you did for the Triscombe farms; it took courage to play the boy and the young man when you were torn from your family. It might not have been very conventional, but I love you for a lot of things, Maxine. Will you believe me and forgive me for calling my love my "regard"? I was trying not to rush you.'

She sighed happily. 'We have so much explaining to do, Rupert, but I do think we should go and tell Grandmama.'

'Just one more kiss.'

A little while later and with the arrangement of Maxine's dress to acceptable standards of decency, they made their way back into Lidiard Grange.

The dowager had been waiting impatiently for their return. As they entered the drawing-room, she took one look at their faces.

'Congratulations,' she said happily. 'I am very pleased.'